DEAD FLOWERS

DEAD FLOWERS

ALEXANDER LAIDLAW

Stories

NIGHTWOOD EDITIONS

2019

Nightwood Editions
P.O. Box 1779
Gibsons, BC VON 1VO
Canada
www.nightwoodeditions.com

COVER DESIGN: Topshelf Creative
TYPOGRAPHY: Carleton Wilson

 Canada Council   Conseil des Arts
for the Arts   du Canada

Nightwood Editions acknowledges the support of the Canada Council for the Arts, which last year invested $153 million to bring the arts to Canadians throughout the country.

Nous remercions le Conseil des arts du Canada de son soutien. L'an dernier, le Conseil a investi 153 millions de dollars pour mettre de l'art dans la vie des Canadiennes et des Canadiens de tout le pays.

We also gratefully acknowledge financial support from the Government of Canada and from the Province of British Columbia through the BC Arts Council and the Book Publishing Tax Credit.

This book has been produced on 100% post-consumer recycled, ancient-forest-free paper, processed chlorine-free and printed with vegetable-based dyes.

Printed and bound in Canada.

LIBRARY AND ARCHIVES CANADA CATALOGUING IN PUBLICATION

Title: Dead flowers / Alexander Laidlaw.

Names: Laidlaw, Alexander, 1985- author.

Description: Short stories.

Identifiers: Canadiana (print) 20189047887 | Canadiana (ebook) 20189047895 | ISBN 9780889713550 (softcover) | ISBN 9780889711457 (ebook)

Classification: LCC PS8623 A3938 D43 2019 | DDC C813/.6—dc23

in time I will offer one book dedicated
to each and every person I love
as for this book
it doesn't seem right for them
so I give it to the past, wherever it went

CONTENTS

DEAD FLOWERS

It was three o'clock in the morning when I finished a second draft of my letter to Councilman Kane, written because I'd read recently in the news that his wife was dead. *It's such a shame*, I wrote. *She was just such a beautiful woman. I mean, besides whatever else she must have been.* The truth is, I had only ever seen her photo in the papers. *But councilman, it pays to see the good in a bad situation. The whole wide world thinks life is cheap, and really that's the only way to think of it. In the end we are better to have thrown it off. Better that she was able to do it on her own terms and in her own time.* At the end of the letter I signed off saying, *Up, up and away!* After that I fell asleep, sitting upright in my chair.

When I awoke it was morning, and I found myself lying in bed. And it's for reasons like this that I hate this utterly miserable time of the year. Nothing holds together or makes any sense. Everything starts to unravel. I can't even hold myself together, as every thread is now cut so that I can't even trust I'll wake up in the place where I fell asleep.

After waking I lay in bed for hours doing nothing, like a rabbit, with my head in my hands. For hours I looked at the window. Outside the rain was falling, and every so often a little black bird flitted in and out of view. Grape vines, already wasted by the cold, still clung to the garden trellises.

Earlier, Joe had had his friends in for coffee, and there'd been a ruckus above. I knew all about it because of my dreams. It had been the end of the Second World War. Grizzled voices shouted in broken English over the radio. Eyes blinded in a smoke of cigarettes. Tears were shed. There was a tumbling down the stairs. I dreamt of Joe standing under the window, yelling to someone, saying something about plums. He held a pyramid of golden-purple plums in his outstretched hands. But his hands were, as always, covered in dirt. And Joe was, as always, drunk. Coffee in the morning meant three fat fingers of rum spilled into every cup. It was the same thing every Wednesday, he and his friends starting in around seven o'clock.

But don't you think of judging him. Not anymore, you haven't the right. You forfeited that when you left and forgot that Joe was here, was still alive, still putting in hours, still shaking his legs. Just as you forgot this house, this room, this bed, all now still as it was.

By the time I was up, his friends had gone and in all probability, Joe had taken a bus downtown to wet his whistle at the Old Tin Flute, or the Legion, or the Barrel & Bull. And that's another thing I just can't stand about this time of year: the silence, with no sign of life. Only dozens of pots and pans laid out in the yard to catch the rain. And the hot sound of blood roaring in my open ears like a ringing of bells. Which is maybe why I'm writing these letters, these words. Because I do get lonely, understand? And I go crazy with this loneliness. I get out of bed.

I take out the trash. I eat a piece of buttered toast with coffee. I go outside to smoke yet another cigarette, standing in the cold, and I wander barefoot up and down the muddy byways of the garden.

Every year Joe tends his garden. He grows an array of both flowers and food. Every year he overwhelms his neighbours and friends with apples, plums, figs, onions, beans, peas and bunches of kale. But then every year, around this time, the garden up and dies. It leaves him and he flounders. And every year he flounders just a little further off.

I ask him what that's like.

He says, It's exactly like I lost my wife.

More than anything else he misses the flowers, he says, and wishes every year they'd be a bit quicker coming back.

But Joe isn't sentimental. He wears a baseball cap that reads, *Old as Dirt*. All day, every day, he walks around town drunk, his zipper collapsed, and with the soiled tails of his shirt sticking out like a tuft of feathers from the seat of his pants. He calls me a son of a bitch and asks, Don't you ever get tired of fucking only yourself? Then he boasts that he's been growing food for over seventy years, ever since he was nine. I know everything there is to know, he says, his face right close to mine.

It's a story I have heard before, at least half a dozen times. About how his father left to fight in the war, and his brothers left to fight in the war, and the war raged all around, to east and west and north and south. So Joe had to learn to work the land or else see himself, his mother and his sisters starve. In fact, the only piece of the story I had never heard before was something Joe told me this afternoon, about how one of his brothers never came home. According to the army, the brother's body was lost, and the only thing the family ever had of their fallen son was a postcard. It came by mail on a day many months after the boy was supposed to have died. It was addressed to the mother, saying only, *I miss you darling, please come home.*

I said to Joe, That doesn't make sense.

Then he started in asking for rent.

Tonight I sit at the desk, staring into the distance, through the walls and into the night. All around me are scattered pages, the detritus of so many nights I have spent this way. Old ideas and worthless thoughts. Letters that will never be written. Letters written that will never be sent. And all the while I know that the only thing I ought to write, that the one and only thing that could make any difference anymore, would be a letter to you.

I pick up a pen, but nothing comes to mind. Well, it isn't nothing, only it doesn't really make any sense. I mean, it isn't something you'll understand, not now that our lives have split and have come undone and we find ourselves so far apart. You won't understand. You will think one thing, but the truth will be something different. Still, there are no other words I can write.

So I bend myself one more time into the task. I scratch a few words onto the page. Single draft. I'll send it in the morning. *I miss you darling, please come home.*

ONE TIME I WITNESSED
A MURDER

It seems like such a while ago now, but it still comes up in conversation—around the table at a dinner party for instance—and then whoever hasn't heard the story before will want to hear it, and those who have heard it will want me to tell it again.

All eyes on me, I'll reach for a bottle of wine to fill my glass. I don't want to tell it again. I've told this story so many times over the years, but I've never felt I got it right. You just can't talk to people and tell them the truth. Not around the table at a party. Not after so many glasses of wine.

I was a student on summer break after my second or third year at university. I get mixed up remembering the timing, but at any rate it was the summer I decided that from then on I was only going to be a student part-time. It would take me a little longer to earn my degree, but that was fine. What was the point, anyway, of working so hard to finish school? Four years of hard work to be followed by what? Hard work the rest of your life.

I didn't even have a job at the time. Until recently, I had been a cook at an upscale Italian place, but then one day I simply walked out. Actually, what happened is I got drunk one night and then slept through my morning alarm. By the time I woke up, I had missed my shift, so I never went back.

My girlfriend was having her doubts about me. We were supposed to take a trip that summer. We'd talked about going to Portland, or maybe north to the Yukon to camp. We hadn't yet figured it out, but when a friend of mine offered me a ride to the Calgary Stampede, saying that he also had a place for me to stay, I said I would go. There wasn't any room in the car for my girlfriend, but I failed to see the connection between this development and our nascent plans. She was angry with me when I told her the news. This means we won't take a trip of our own, she said.

I said, Ayleen, the summer is long. There'll still be plenty of time for us to get away.

But you won't have any money, she said.

Well, I couldn't argue with that.

That summer, she and I were living together—though it is more accurate to say I was living with her. The room had been Ayleen's before I had come, and it would be hers again after I left. I kept all my things in a very neat pile apart from everything else in the room. But we did have a cat together, sort of. The cat had belonged to somebody else in the building but was neglected. Ayleen and I had taken to feeding the poor thing, so finally the little beast came to live in our room.

And we had a nice little life together, I thought, she and I and the cat in that room. I would open the door onto the balcony to let in the air and the light. Ayleen would dangle a bit of yarn for the cat. The cat would jump, and I would take a picture of that—her legs and the light and the cat and the yarn.

But then I went away to Calgary and was drunk for three days and nights. Ayleen planned a trip of her own to visit family and friends up the coast. When I got back, she was already gone.

I woke up, and it was already noon. I made a cup of coffee and took it on the balcony. Our railings were overgrown with vines coming up from the garden below. Some of it was clematis, but mostly morning glory. It was mid-July and those flowers had started to bloom. It never rained much during the summer, so lawns throughout the city were scorched. It was sunny almost every day and hot, but at night a chilling moisture would descend.

And that was that city—that was July.

This is the story I don't ever get to tell. These are the poignant details, not about the body, not about the blood, but the real and significant-or-not details I never get to mention. Like how on that first day without her I didn't eat breakfast but had a coffee then drank a beer. I immediately felt guilty for drinking the beer. I felt as if someone was watching. I felt as if I might get caught.

But at least I hadn't *planned* on drinking a beer after coffee that day. I had simply been going through my knapsack and had found a can of lager left over from Calgary. So I drank it and then felt ashamed. I felt shaky and even slightly buzzed. I felt terrible actually, miserable, and I thought I should eat something but I had no appetite. So instead of eating I rode my bicycle downtown, parked it at the library and spent the rest of that day hiding out in the stacks, covering my many moral failings with a conspicuous effort to expand the horizons of my learning.

Later that night I wanted to write. I felt I had to organize the contents of my head. I was sick at heart, which in those days always led me to paper and pen. I cleared a space for myself at Ayleen's desk. It was dark outside and I could see the reflection of myself in her bedroom window. I set out my notebook and pen. I made a coffee to keep myself awake.

I'm in love with a woman who doesn't love me, I wrote, because that was what seemed to be true. *There's probably some other man in her life. Someone to indicate all of my faults. Or worse, someone to forget me by. She's felt drawn to him and was for a time so loyal to me, she didn't recognize her feelings. Lately though, more so, she thinks about him. It's probably someone she knows from work.*

I put down my pen and thought of Ayleen and the place where she worked. It was an organic market downtown, and she worked as a server in the deli there. She hated her job—or was she fond of it? I suddenly realized that I didn't know. And I felt like a terrible boyfriend, being unsure about this pivotal fact.

I picked up my pen.

While I'd been away, Ayleen had gone out one night with her friends from work. They'd all gone to a bar to see some show, and of course the man in question had been there. Probably there had been dancing, first part of a larger group before the two of them found each other, gradually, each little step taken toward one another, each unremarkable if considered alone. And probably he had walked her home. Same thing—beginning with five or six individuals heading northeast, leaving downtown, then each of the others falling away until the two of them stood at the swinging iron gate at the foot of our stairs.

I wrote this as I imagined it could have happened. Nothing outrageous at first. *She stands on the bottom stair, turns to him, says, Well, goodnight?* I recorded the rise of a blush, not in her face but in the upper pallet of her breasts. Her blush for knowing, even if not admitting yet, the thing this all was building toward. *He watches her legs on the stairs. She moves slowly, giving him the pleasure of this, teasing him, drawing him on.* Slowly, taking me hours to get to the place of *her body and his in our sheets.*

Why? would be a reasonable question. Why would I want to create such a scene? Because I was feeling shaky, uncertain, unwell and I wanted to make myself crazy that night. And I did go half-crazy that night, laying her to bed with another in prose.

The next day, I woke up around noon. I made a cup of coffee and took it on the balcony.

Now, if I could truly tell this story how I wanted, I would want to take a few moments here to talk about something else entirely.

I remember the cat was called Munich, but we wanted to change its name to Munch, after the artist Edvard Munch. I wasn't a fan of Munch and as far as I know, neither was Ayleen. But some weeks before we abducted the cat, we'd found a Norwegian film about the artist at the library and brought it home to watch it one night. It was such a long movie, and so terribly slow and strange. Every so often a character would break from their scene and look directly at the camera, at the viewer. It was disconcerting, as if something had been said that we hadn't understood and now a response was demanded of us.

The movie was so long that we had to take a break midway through. We had to walk to the store and back to stretch our legs and to fortify ourselves with a snack before braving the second half. It was probably three o'clock in the morning by the time we finished it and I don't know why, but we were wired, wide awake, full of a nervous energy. Was it something in the subject of the film that had infected us? Or was this simply an effect of having been held for so long at the pace of the film that we found ourselves with an untimely quantity of pent-up energy? We didn't know what to do, but knew we had to get out—out of our bed, out of the room, into the city and into the night. We tied up our laces and left, and that night we walked together and talked for three, four, five, six hours. God knows. We got back to the room and fell into bed and made love until both of us slept, even into our sleep trying to continue the act.

So of course we wanted to change the name of the cat from Munich to Munch. We wanted that cat to be a reminder of just what we were, what we meant to each other. Because yes, we were in love, but we were also so painfully, stupidly young.

The first three days I was alone, and every night I was alone. I didn't go out, didn't see anyone. I was up late sitting at Ayleen's desk, writing out terrible things. About her giving herself to him in ways that the rote of our relationship prevented. About her being lost in him, growing in new directions through a process of abandon, moving into spaces I could neither provide nor follow her into to witness this growth. I made myself sick and aroused writing about her and this man, this unknown man, this man I had never met, this man who in hindsight likely didn't exist.

Then it happened—this murder, the so-called main event. It occurred at the end of a long night wherein I had gotten drunk at a birthday party. My friend Miller had turned twenty-two and he hosted a barbecue to celebrate. I went along more or less for a change of scenery, to get out of her room and away from myself and the rut I had been digging.

Miller lived in one of those rental houses so common around colleges and universities. An old Victorian home carved into so many bedrooms, that had been allowed to slide into disrepair. There were ten to twenty people in every room of the house, wearing shoes and tracking dirt onto the carpets, spilling drinks and leaving half-finished food on tables, shelves and a mantle in the hall. I got drunk off a bottle of wine and then went around picking up stray cans of beer.

The sun went down and the chill set in, then there were people talking about wanting to start a fire in the living room. Someone said, I don't think the fireplace works. Someone else started gathering sticks from the yard. Someone thought to open a window, as the grate was being packed full of kindling and paper. Finally, word went around the room that the birthday boy wanted to leave. There wouldn't be time for any fire. Miller wanted to move everyone to a bar. But what bar? Not just any. Miller wanted to see a woman take her clothes off and dance.

Soon we were all packed into cars, heading to some club with a depressingly large parking lot. It was already late by the time we arrived, so there was only one woman left to dance. She was sexy though, and wasted no time getting out of her clothes. She didn't look unhappy, either. She looked like she believed in the good of her body, as if she wanted to share it, though that couldn't be true. We were crowded around the stage, the only people in the room, the party of us now dwindled to fifteen, maybe ten.

After the club, there was nothing more to do since it was now so late and the bars downtown would be closed. Somebody suggested we return to the house. For my part, I thought of going home. I thought of climbing up the stairs into Ayleen's room, of undressing myself, falling into her bed. Too drunk to get to sleep, I thought I'd probably wind up touching myself, if I could even get hard.

And in that moment, such a mess of imagery crashed into my psyche—of all the things I had imagined these past few days, now mingling with the body of the dancer. Somehow over everything, the thought of my own nudity soiling our bed was too much for me, somehow proof and a symbol of irreparable sin. Better to go on, I thought.

So as the last stragglers entered a car headed back to Miller's house, I squeezed into the back seat, trying to make myself small and inconspicuous. I didn't leave his place until everyone else had either gone or fallen sleep. Miller himself was the first to retire, slipping into unconsciousness on the couch with a glass of Antiguan rum in his hand. A woman named Chelsea then talked for maybe an hour about China, about the rise of the East, about the trade deficit, about Falun Gong and smog over the cities of Beijing, Tianjin, Shandong, Henan.

When I did go, I forgot all about my bicycle. I left it leaning against the side of the house and set off on foot. I was tired and I was angry. In those days, I'd sometimes get angry for no discernable reason. Once I even tried to throw a rock through a storefront window, just because I was angry, walking by myself at night.

I had nothing against the store, nor the window. I'd just been walking around with a big rock in my hand, carrying it through the city streets, all the while waiting until I'd gathered up enough nerve to try and break something. Because I was angry, I just wanted to see something broken. And so, I threw the rock like a discus into the tall and likely tempered sheet of glass. Luckily, it didn't break. The rock hit the glass, made a noise like thunder, and I ran off down the street.

Where did this anger originate? I don't know. It would come on suddenly like the sting of a wasp. Luckily, I was always alone when it happened. Always alone and usually drunk and walking around at night. Maybe it was simply because I was drunk and alone, because it was late and I had a long way to go. Or maybe it came on because I was just twenty or twenty-one years old, and already felt sick and cheated by life. Maybe it was because I felt I had very little control over what life would become.

One thing was certain—it would never get any better than this. I was young and it was summer and I didn't have a job. School was easy and paid for. And on top of everything else, there was this beautiful, charming young woman who allowed me to stay with her, to live in her room and to share her bed for only the cost of love. So I was basically just waiting for things to get worse, and I thought that there was no way I could stop it. It seems petty now, juvenile, but maybe that's what made me feel so angry back then.

That night I had a long way to walk. At one point I heard an argument that sounded as if it would break into violence as I approached. There was a group of men up ahead on the opposite side of the street. Maybe two, maybe more, seemed ready to fight. I checked to see if there were any cars coming, but the road was empty so I crossed. I wanted to walk right into the fray. Maybe I'll get accosted, I thought. The chance of this appealed to me. Maybe I'll even get punched. Likely it'd do me some good.

But by the time I reached them, the argument had died out. The men were quiet and let me pass without any hassle. I felt ridiculous for having wanted to be harmed. What was this about, this mood I had been nurturing?

I started thinking about Ayleen—the manner in which I had made use of her, and the idea of her during the past few days. It all seemed ridiculous now. This twisted fantasy I had endeavoured to build, her infidelity—that wasn't her. That was just me trying to fuck with myself. But to what purpose? I wondered. What did I gain out of trying to torture myself?

Just then, to the side of the road, I noticed a garden full of pointed green shrubs that looked just like pineapple tops. Growing out of each of these pineapple tops was a vertical bough totally covered in white-coloured, bell-shaped flowers. I know now that those were yucca plants and yucca flowers, but back then I didn't know anything. I was simply enamoured—because by now the sky was growing purple, and those flowers were so startlingly bright.

I decided in an instant to forgive myself those past few days, and not only that, but to forgive all other failings I'd been carrying. Whatever negativity was in me, I was going to let it go. I was going to break off one of these boughs and I was going to carry it home and give it to Ayleen. She'd be coming back the next day from her trip. I stepped into the garden, reached into one of those plants, and snapped its bough off near the ground. The thing was as long as my arm, a whole shock of white flowers, and I carried it the rest of the way home.

Near to where we lived, across the street in fact, was an elementary school. With the direction I had followed that night, it made sense for me to take a shortcut through the schoolyard. There was a hole in the fence at the far end of the field that let out right across from our gate.

As I was rounding the corner of the school building, I saw movement to my left and turned to look. I saw what seemed to be a woman bending over the body of a man on the ground. The man was on his back and appeared to be unconscious. The woman, or maybe she was a girl—she looked small next to the man—was busy lifting up his legs and trying to drag him. There were some bushes growing in a planter box next to the entrance of the school, and it looked like she was going to try to hide him there. I saw all of this in single glance, and then I looked away and kept walking.

All summer I had noticed a small homeless population at the school. It was a short walk here from downtown, so I supposed it made a decent place to crash and spend the night. There were plenty of corners, shadows, nooks, and there was cover, too, in case it ever rained. But it didn't rain that summer, and people had been sleeping more or less in the open all around the building. It was a good place to sleep, but also seemed a decent spot to shoot up.

When I saw the man lying on the ground, I figured he'd had an overdose. And I guessed the girl had got scared and was now trying to make him disappear. I didn't think the man was dead. In fact, I thought I might save the man's life if I only kept walking. The girl was going to leave, I thought, and then I would double back to check on him. I only had to keep my eyes averted, and not let on to the girl that I had noticed her.

My plan failed in a number of ways. First, I couldn't keep my eyes averted. The next time I glanced at the scene, the girl had spotted me. Of course she'd spotted me. I was carrying a bough of bright white flowers half the size of my body, aloft in the air. By then she'd got the man into the bushes. She'd left him and was walking toward me.

I thought about dropping to my belly. We were still far enough apart, and enough darkness remained of the night perhaps to cover me. But I was too nervous, or the gesture seemed dramatic. Instead I kept on walking. I kept moving forward and didn't look back.

I was halfway across the field when I finally gathered the nerve to turn around. The girl was gone, having probably taken a different exit through another part of the fence.

At that point I went back to check on the man. He was clearly dead. His neck had been cut. The ground over which he'd been dragged was covered in blood. Because the girl had been pulling him from the ankles, his shirt had ridden up from his body to cover his face. I didn't touch him. I didn't get close to him. There was no point. There was nothing I could do.

Later, I'd been taken to the police station. They had me waiting around for a detective to come in for the morning shift. I sat in an interrogation room. I tried to sleep but couldn't. All I wanted was a pillow and a blanket. Instead someone gave me cold coffee and a muffin. I was interviewed by Detective Emerald Tucker. He was grey-haired, round and not unkind. He asked if he could tape our conversation.

I want you to tell me what you did last night, said Detective Tucker. Start with the evening. Proceed chronologically and tell me everything you can remember. Don't worry if it seems like there's no connection between what you have to say and the event you witnessed. Take your time. Lead into the morning, and only then tell me what you witnessed at the school.

I told him about the birthday party, about Miller having turned twenty-two. I told him about the bottle of wine and the beer I'd had to drink, about the club and the girl who had danced across the stage. I told him it had been sad to witness her dancing, though it hadn't been sad at the time. Now it seems sad, I told him. Then I tried to recount all of what Chelsea had said about China as the tape recorder rolled on.

Detective Tucker listened closely, as if the key to solving this crime might somehow lay within the scattered bulk of these details. When it came to describing my walk home, I told him about the men who had been arguing, on the verge of fighting, and he didn't seem surprised to hear that I'd wanted to get beaten up. But when I talked about the flowers, he became curious. What happened to those flowers, he wanted to know.

I hadn't thought about it. I must have dropped them on the floor when I got home.

That was when you dialled 911? he asked. You live alone?

I live with my girlfriend, I said, and a cat.

Where was she?

My girlfriend? She's out of town.

And how long have you two been together?

About a year, I said. Or no—two years.

Detective Tucker paused and studied me a moment. Did anything else happen before you reached the school? Did you run into anyone else? he asked.

I told him how I had shared a cigarette with a fellow who was high on mushrooms.

Were you high on anything last night?

No, I said. Not me—the other guy. I was sitting down to take a break from walking when he went by and I asked him if he had a cigarette he could spare. He said he didn't have one to spare, but that we could share one. I said okay, so then he stopped and we smoked and chatted for a minute.

The fellow told me he was going to his friend's place, that there were three naked women just hanging out at his friend's apartment, and that actually come to think of it, he didn't have time to be standing around smoking cigarettes and chatting with me. After that he took off in a hurry down the street.

The last question the detective asked was whether or not I had killed that man.

No, I said. Then I said it again in a different way, just to be certain I hadn't misspoken.

He said, Understand that I have to ask you this question, but why should I believe you?

After the interview, the police took my clothes and my shoes and entered them into evidence. They gave me a polyester suit to wear, much like a vacuum-cleaner bag with a zipper up the front. Detective Tucker drove me home in his personal car. As we pulled away from the station he asked if I'd mind if he lit a cigarette.

My wife doesn't know that I smoke, he said. But I've been smoking every day for nearly twenty years. I only ever do it with the windows down, and I only ever do it before lunch.

More or less, that's the end of the story. There is more I could say, but it rambles outward from this point. One time I witnessed a murder, but I didn't see anything I hadn't already seen. I mean, it was the same basic material as what makes up this life, only rearranged, temporary laid out differently for the sake of creating some shock and awe. I didn't witness the death of a man, because I didn't know the man, and so to me he wasn't real. I didn't see the hand that dealt the blow. I didn't see the blade that cut the skin. Once again though, I fear that I'm not telling it right. I should stick to things that can be explained.

Ayleen was to come home later that day. I waited for her and couldn't sleep. I wanted to break for her, to fall apart and weep into her arms when she arrived because when I got back to our room, I really was reeling and was in a kind of shock. I didn't want to be alone. I wanted Ayleen. I wanted her to come and make everything right. So much had been wrong and I thought it would do us both good if I could only fall apart for her, if I could just collapse and be a mess for her the moment she came in through the door.

But the waiting was long. I couldn't hold out. I couldn't stand to be alone that day, so I rented a pile of movies. By the time Ayleen walked into the room I had already watched three dumb movies back to back. I had ordered a pizza and felt sick. I was tired and distracted, so I didn't collapse, but I told her what happened.

And later that evening, already forgetting and blurring the truth, I told her again.

ON GORDON HEAD

Elly hated flying, but there was something about flying west. That feeling of having been up since the world was dark, of having boarded a plane, of having been in the air for what seemed already like the bulk of a day only to land and find it was hardly noon. That the sun was full and bright when she felt it should be setting. Flying west always made her feel buoyed for the day and estranged, the way she thought a sleepwalker would.

Elly took a bus downtown and transferred, headed for the university. As the bus pulled up at a stop in front of the Student Union Building, she saw Sam on a bench with a paperback. He was wearing sunglasses, jeans and a black T-shirt. The sunglasses, she thought, were too big for his face.

She tried to sneak up on him, but Sam was so eager he kept looking up from his book. He spotted her, and his mouth spread into a wide, involuntary grin.

They hugged and she told him, Your legs are shaking.

That's because I'm nervous, said Sam.

You're nervous? Really?

They kissed.

On separating, Elly asked, What are you reading?

I wasn't really reading. I was waiting for you.

Oh, well that's sweet, she said, but looking over his shoulder anyway she saw that the book was by Anaïs Nin. A slim novella lying flat on a narrow, wooden bench.

They caught a cab to the house where Elly had rented a room. She had rented it sight-unseen, had found the ad online, and had spoken to a guy named Jim over the phone one day. The situation was less than perfect, but being as it was so hard to find a place near campus this time of year, Elly had been willing to accept anything.

The cab took them into a neighbourhood sloped, falling toward the shore. The trees overhead loomed larger here, their branches reaching over the road.

Elly sat with her legs crossed, leaning back and trying not to smile. Sam was beaming though, looking at her from across the back seat. He even reached out to touch her on the knee, as if to be assured that this wasn't a dream.

The house was white and overgrown with moss. It seemed that the front of it hardly got any sun. Elly's room would be in the basement, but now with the help of Sam she lugged her suitcases up the front steps. She rang the bell and a big black dog came barking from out of the living room. She heard a voice say, Don't mind him, and then saw someone rise from the couch.

Jim opened the door and introduced himself. He held the dog by its collar, but only to prevent it from running out. Once Elly and Sam were inside, he let go. The dog rubbed its face excitedly against their legs and wagged its tail.

This is Banjo, said Jim. He's friendly. And then speaking to the dog said, C'mon boy. Leave it, leave them alone.

Jim had the look of a child who had grown up too fast. His body was sort of shapeless, undefined, but his face looked tired. Ushering them into the living room and taking his place on the couch again, Jim explained that Elly had chosen an excellent day to arrive.

Just last night, he said, we had to evict a guy out of the basement, because he lost his mind and tried to kill my dog, all because Banjo got into his room and ate a couple granola bars. The guy had chased the dog around the house, said Jim, with a hunting knife. We had to call the cops, and we only finally got him out of here at four in the morning.

Jim showed them Elly's room. It was a space downstairs with grey carpet, white walls and a window facing the front. As soon as they were alone again, Sam approached.

Not here, Elly said. It's too dusty and weird.

Well, where should we go? asked Sam.

I don't know. We have nowhere to go.

After dropping her luggage, Elly and Sam set off on foot to explore the neighbourhood. Neither of them had ever lived in this area, although they'd been here for parties before. In their memories it was always winter here, always wet and dark. It was always late and they were lost on a kind of fool's errand trying to find their way out.

It was the end of the summer though, and the sun was full and bright as they walked away from Elly's house. Veering into a lane at the end of her street, they soon found themselves at the mouth of a trail. The trail brought them onto the ocean, but instead of on a beach, they found themselves standing over a low bank of cliffs with long grass and shrubs growing out of the rock. The cliffs were rounded, as if the rock itself was caught in a motion of falling, bending forward, slipping its head beneath the waves.

Elly and Sam had been apart for some months. Each of them had been waiting for a moment like this. Now that they were alone and in relative privacy, they fell into each other on the rocks. Elly was on top and then they rolled, and although they couldn't take off any clothes, they pressed into each other. Sam used the buckle of his belt to bear into her, and Elly felt soft, as if the bones had gone out of her body. She felt pliable and kneaded, caught between the spine of a rock and the callous urgency of a man she thought she loved.

Elly started setting up her room. She found a desk and dresser at the Sally Anne and procured a futon frame and a mattress from relatives. Sam helped her carry these things home, carting everything on the bus and taking multiple trips.

She complained one day of having only one set of bedsheets so Jim showed her a closet in the house full of linens. She asked him who they belonged to and he shrugged. They'd been left behind, abandoned, he said, so Elly took a selection of the best. She washed them twice and let them air out in the sun.

All over the house were the signs and remnants of previous tenants. One couldn't make sense or remember the history of all those who'd lived in these rooms. In the kitchen, taking up a portion of the table, was a sprawling collection of unopened mail. The collection was several years old and continued to grow, all because someone in the house had decided it was unlawful to either open or discard another person's mail. So here was a pile of envelopes, each one addressed to one of a litany of names. Elly, over breakfast one day, tried to organize the pile. She counted twenty-five different names before her tea had grown cold, but in the end she gave up.

Of the people who lived here now, besides Jim, there were three living upstairs. Tom and Julia shared a room, although the room belonged to Julia, and then there was Sara. Downstairs, there were two other bedrooms besides the one that Elly rented. The one that had belonged to Banjo's would-be killer remained empty for now. The other was where Jodi lived. Jodi was a friend of Tom's and she owned two dogs. Julia also had a dog. So, thought Elly, counting it out, six bedrooms, one empty, six people, four dogs.

Elly learned more about the house from both Jim and Tom. These two men, each a few years older than her, were both similar and yet different from each other. She hardly ever saw the two of them together. It was as if they traded shifts. During the day, every day, it would be Tom sitting in the living room, watching TV with Julia's dog at his feet and Banjo on the edges of the room. Then the sun would set and suddenly it'd be Jim, sitting on the couch, beer in his hand, Banjo at his feet, the other dog now a respectful distance off.

There was a rhythm to each one of her roommates, Elly soon learned. Sara, for instance, was pre-med and on weekends she liked to get drunk. She worked hard in school and pushed herself, but also kept a vibrant social life. She had several men in her life, although none was ever seen around the house. Often, Sara would disappear from Thursday morning until Sunday night, and then be found in the kitchen, sheepishly making herself a meal, nursing a headache with Tylenol, and getting ready to shuffle off early to bed.

Julia was studying law. She shared a bedroom with Tom, but the bedroom was hers, and the lease for the entire house was in her name. Elly hadn't met her yet. She could hear Julia in the morning though, leaving the house at an impossibly early hour. Then again at night as Julia returned home after dark. The woman drove a vintage Oldsmobile which made such an awful racket, Elly could hardly fail to notice her coming and going.

Every morning Julia would get up and shower. Meanwhile, Tom would put the coffee on. She would pour herself a cup, give Tom a quick kiss and give her dog a quick pat on the head. The two of them would stand together in the doorway, looking lost and forlorn, watching her go. Elly imagined that the dog would be the first to lose interest as Julia's car disappeared. The dog would slink back into the house, find its place in the living room and wait for Tom.

Tom was not a student and he didn't have a job. Until recently, he'd been in Alberta working on the oil sands, and because his work had been seasonal, he collected what amounted to a generous wage in unemployment checks.

It was hard to imagine Tom on the oil sands. He wore rectangular glasses and had long and somewhat wavy blond hair. He spoke with a lisp and didn't seem to have friends. So, between caring for his girlfriend's bedroom and her dog, he had plenty of time to sit and think.

Tom wasn't unhappy. He was patient and calm. He was even puritanical, in a way. He admitted to Elly that he'd once been hooked on methamphetamines, but that these days coffee was his only vice. Through diet, focus and daily contemplation, he was trying to maintain a healthy body, mind and soul.

When Elly and Julia finally met, Elly was just waking up from a nap. It was the middle of the day and she'd been lying on the couch. Meanwhile, Julia had only come into the house for a moment, running in just to run out again.

Elly heard voices and opened her eyes. Tom was at the door with a woman who was thin, with a sharp nose and long blond hair. Seeing that Elly had opened her eyes, and that she was trying hard to stay awake, Julia smiled. She said to Tom, Oh, isn't she a pretty young thing?

Meeting Sara, Elly got another distinct perspective on life in the house. Sara informed her that everyone here (herself excluded, naturally) suffered from genital warts.

It's just something to think about, Sara said, that there is a certain amount of hygienic discretion you'll want to uphold.

Another helpful tip was to never leave any used tampons in the bathroom because, according to Sara, Banjo couldn't help himself. He's a fucking mutt, she explained. Somehow, he gets into the room, sticks his nose into the bin, and then spreads them around the house.

Elly continued to settle in her room. She dusted, cleaned the walls, vacuumed the carpet, washed the window. She had an issue with the window, in that it wouldn't open. She wished it would, and it seemed as if it had been made to open, so she tested it. She pressed her fingers into the glass and pushed, but it was stuck.

Elly kept waiting for a run-in with Jodi. Every time she opened her bedroom door, she was prepared to see Jodi in the hallway. She expected to see Jodi at the shared washing machine, outside the bathroom, or to see her standing in the basement kitchenette, hovering over the stove with a mug, waiting for water to boil. But a week went by, then another week, and still she hadn't met her final roommate.

Even more unlikely was that there were two dogs living in Jodi's room, and that Elly had neither seen nor heard any hint of them. Elly pressed her ear against the wall and thought she heard the jiggling of a collar, maybe the intake of a breath.

Finally one morning, as she was making herself a bit of toast, Elly heard a scuffling of paws over the floor, then the sticky sound of a door being opened. All of a sudden the dogs came bounding into the room, overwhelming her. They tumbled together and were practically jumping over one another on their way toward the door in a corner of the little kitchenette. The door opened onto a staircase that went up into the yard. The dogs waited there, hardly able to contain themselves. One was bouncing up and down on its forepaws, the other was shaking, waiting for her master.

Jodi came into the room and smiled wearily. She opened the door, allowing the dogs to burst up the stairs. Once in the yard, they squatted to piss in the uncut grass.

Jodi stood in the open doorway and lit a cigarette. She rubbed her eyes. She was wearing colourful, kitschy pajama pants, a faded tank top without a bra, and had a tangle of wild orange hair.

You must be Eleanor, Jodi said.

Oh, it's Elizabeth, actually.

Jodi looked her up and down. Well, that is a much better name, she said.

The dogs were running in rapid circles around and around the yard. Elly knew nothing about dogs. She would have said that one of these was maybe a greyhound, but it probably wasn't.

It looked like it was made to run though. It was fast and lean and strong. Jodi introduced the dogs as Franny and Zooey.

Oh funny. Which one is the boy? Elly asked.

No, said Jodi, they're girls. And then after a pause, You're a student?

I am. I'm studying anthropology, I think. I mean, that's what I'm doing now, but it might change. It'll probably change.

Well, Jodi replied, you're young anyway.

Right, so I guess I get to change my mind.

Having already spoken about Jodi with Tom, Elly knew a bit about her past. She knew that Jodi had grown up in Prince George, that she had moved to Vancouver as a teenager, that she had attempted some college, but eventually decided it wasn't for her. Now she worked part-time as a dispatch person for the local police. Elly tried to imagine Jodi wearing a headset, sitting at a cramped desk and taking emergency calls, pushing buttons on a complicated phone. Jodi's other job, which she worked full-time, was at Starbucks. Jodi explained that her hours were long. She started early and finished late, which is probably why Elly hadn't seen her before. As for the dogs, they stayed kennelled in her room whenever Jodi was out.

I used to let them run around in there, she said, but they peed all over and Franny, I think it was Franny, tore the place up. I came home once and found that she had chewed up a box of my old photographs, so that was the last time I had them out. Because that was my life, you know. All my memories, Jodi made a gesture, gone.

After talking a while, Jodi stepped into the yard. She sat at the top of the stairs and crossed her legs. The dogs came to see her. The one, the runner, was grey. The other was white. The grey one jumped and tried to lick her face. Jodi pushed it away with her fingertips, but then as an afterthought, scooped its jaw into the palm of her hand and held it tenderly.

For a while, living in that room, Elly was eager to open the window. She thought that she could possibly hire someone to come and work the thing onto some hinges. Sam thought she was crazy.

Listen to you, talk about hiring someone. Do you have any idea what that's going to cost? he asked.

Sympathetic as he was though to her every desire, Sam remembered that he knew a guy who had worked on a construction crew.

Maybe we could ask him for advice, he said.

The advice was to take off the window's trim, then run a knife between the window and the wall to find where it was fastened, or nailed. Once the nails had been found, they could be cut with a saw, and then the window could be simply removed.

Okay, Elly said, and then what?

Beats me, said Sam. Buy a new window?

The window was a safety issue, certainly, but Elly's concern with it was primarily aesthetic. She just couldn't stand how the air in the room sat heavy all the time, unmoving. September had come in with a breeze, but within her bedroom, everything was stagnant. There was no flow. Energy was stuck. Everything was bound, caught up in the corners.

And she did spend an hour one afternoon, armed with a butter knife, popping the trim. She crouched on her desk, and as Sam's friend had suggested that it might be possible just to push the window out of the wall with a steady, even force, she laid her shoulder against the frame, but the damned thing wouldn't budge.

With Sam, she spent long days in bed. On weekends they went out on dates. They would sit in a downtown bar drinking beer and cocktails, talking for hours.

One Friday afternoon they met on campus after their classes were done. Sam had asked if Elly would split a sandwich. He had in mind a particular grassy knoll where he thought they might like to sit. Admittedly, it wasn't much of a knoll, just a shaded bit of grass above the sidewalk.

It's alright, Elly said about the knoll, I guess.

Did I rave about the knoll? Did I build it up too much?

After sharing the sandwich, the couple decided to drink a beer at the campus pub. Hours later, as the sun was low and golden, they walked home. That is, they walked the long and winding roads to Elly's house. That night they didn't go out. Instead they remained in bed and played mancala, tired and contented after sex.

Elly said, I've got to rearrange this room.

Sam looked up in a distracted way. I like it, he said, just the way it is.

Ugh, it's suffocating. Just look at this corner, Elly said and jumped out of the bed. I need something to put in this corner, but I don't know what it should be.

Why don't we move the bed over there? That way we could see out the window. Imagine, Sam said, waking up, lying in bed and seeing the sky...

Sure, while everyone else looks in and sees us, Elly said with a snort.

The next day they woke up late and stayed in bed an extra hour or two. As they got up, the afternoon was starting to fade. They ran into Jodi on their way out of the house. It was the first time that Jodi and Sam met.

Introductions were made and Jodi asked, How long have you two been together?

Well it's kind of a long story, Sam started. We met last year, and we spent some time together, but then we were apart. We wrote each other letters almost every day, for four months, but I guess we weren't really a couple until we came back here at the end of the summer.

So, it's basically a month, Elly concluded.

Jodi grinned and waggled her head. I knew you two were fresh because of all the time you spend caged up together in that room.

October came, and Tom moved out. Afterward, Julia's dog almost died. The poor thing didn't eat anything for a week. His body trembled and he looked depressed.

That dog really creeps me out, said Jim. He just stands at the edge of the room and stares. He's like, too intelligent for his own good. I have no fucking clue what must be going through his head.

He's just sad, Elly said. He lost a friend.

Tom and Julia had apparently split. The details would never be known to the rest of the roommates, but Tom had returned to Alberta and his unlikely work on the oil sands. The dog eventually rallied. As for Julia, nothing much changed. She still woke up every day before the sun, had a shower, made a whole pot of coffee for herself, and then drove off noisily in her Oldsmobile. Presumably she worked all day, very focused and diligent, then came home just to sleep. Every so often a friend would come home with her, but he never spent the night. Whether or not it was the same friend every time, Elly couldn't be sure. To her it seemed to make sense this way, although she too had been sad to see Tom disappear. It made sense for Julia to be without his sedentary love lingering around the house. And although nothing was overtly altered, although Julia's schedule and her demeanour remained unchanged, Elly sensed now that she moved with greater ease and balance.

Elly did notice a more distinct change when it came to Sam, however. As they settled into habit, Elly began to feel that their reasons for being together were becoming less obvious. It was as if things were meant to work out between them, if only because of their long separation, if only because of the letters they'd written. Everything should be well and they should be in love. But one night, as they were having sex, Elly felt overwhelmed. Suddenly fed up, she rolled off him.

You have to stop doing that, she said.

Doing what? What are you talking about?

You keep grabbing me, like with your hands on my hips. You keep moving me around the way you want me to move. It's like you don't really want me, you want, like, a doll to fuck.

I don't want a doll, said Sam. Honestly, I didn't know I was doing that.

Well, you do it every time, Elly said, and it feels awful.

I'm sorry, said Sam. Really, I didn't know. I don't want a doll.

A few days later, it was he who lost his patience. This was on a Sunday night after they'd spent a few hours drinking in a bar. Elly and Sam were walking back to his place, when out of the blue, Sam muttered something about not wanting to spend the night together.

What? said Elly. Why?

Because you're drunk.

Elly laughed. I'm drunk? Yeah, but so are you.

Yeah, but it was your idea to go to a bar.

Was it? Elly thought. Had it been her idea? In her recollection, they had made the plan together.

I don't understand why you always want to drink. Every night that we go out, it's like the only thing we do, said Sam.

I didn't, Elly said. I mean, I'm totally surprised by this.

Yeah, said Sam, well. Maybe it's something you should think about.

Sam kept walking. Elly followed. Half a block later, they were walking side by side again. And then, despite what Sam had said, they did spend that night together at his place.

After Tom left the house, a problem arose regarding Jodi's dogs. It seemed that every afternoon, Tom had been taking them out for a walk in the yard. Franny and Zooey had grown accustomed to this, but without Tom, no one was there to let them out. Now, whenever Elly finished classes for the day and returned to her room, the dogs would start to howl in despair. Elly tried to ignore them. She opened a book and lay down in her bed but the dogs kept up a constant, plaintive noise. In the end, she ventured into Jodi's room.

The first time she ever went in there, she found all the windows wide open. It was late October and cold outside. She could almost see her breath. The dogs were quiet, waiting for her. Their kennels were at the far side of the bedroom. Elly had to step over a pile of clothes, and in doing so, felt as if she'd crossed a line. Jodi was a stranger, more or less, but here was her underwear, limp and discarded on top of the pile. Here were her books and her pictures on the wall. And here was Elly, making her way deeper into this more-or-less stranger's life, gingerly crossing the bedroom, trying not to touch or upset anything. When she opened the kennel doors, the dogs bolted out of the room. She followed and found them by the door in the kitchenette. When she let them into the yard, they stopped and squatted to pee. Urine escaped them with such a force, Elly noticed, that it carved little divots in the dirt.

When it was time to bring them in, Elly found that the dogs were well-trained. Sadly, all she had to do was snap her fingers and point, then they bowed their heads and followed. Elly pointed to the door, and they followed down the stairs. She pointed to the bedroom, and they went in. The white dog, Franny, made a bow toward her cage. She folded herself in and laid down, so that Elly only had to shut the gate. Zooey, on the other hand, approached the kennel, but then sat down firmly in front of it. It was as if she understood what had to happen, but she fought against it, even knowing she would lose. Elly tried petting her, tried to gently coax the dog into the box, but Zooey was unbending. She trembled. She wouldn't look at Elly, but kept her eyes fixed on the floor.

Okay, Elly said to the dog. I'm sorry, but I'm going to have to do this.

She took a deep breath and cursed Jodi, then in one swift movement, picked up the mutt by its rump and stuffed its face into the box. But Zooey continued to fight. She dug her forepaws into the floor and pushed back. With her other arm, Elly had to fold the dog's legs. She forced Zooey into the kennel, and then quickly closed the gate before the dog could turn around. After that, she left the room, closed the door and settled back into bed. She picked up a textbook but couldn't read. *What was worse,* she wondered, *the fact that Franny so pathetically accepted being kennelled, or the fact the Zooey fought against it as she did?* Elly tried to focus on her reading, but she had hardly finished half a page before the dogs started howling all over again.

In November, Jodi tried to kill herself. Elly was the only other person in the house. It was reading week, so Sam had gone to visit with his family. Elly had expected an invitation. She had hoped for one, but it hadn't come. Julia and Sara had gone off together on a driving trip with some mutual friends. Even Jim was away, gone who knows where.

It was a Saturday night and Elly had been working on an essay. She'd been holed up in her bedroom reading articles with titles such as, "Irrational Exuberance: Neoliberal subjectivity and the perversion of truth." It was late and she was close to giving up.

Earlier, she'd been out for a walk. Coming home she had found a note on the bathroom door. *Sleeping in the bath tonight,* it had read. *No phone calls please.* Now, lying in bed with the lights out, Elly started thinking about that note. Lately she had noticed that Jodi wasn't well. Elly hardly ever saw her, but she heard her through the walls. She had often heard her arguing with someone on the phone. She had heard her coming and going, all day, all night. Jodi hardly ever seemed to sleep. Elly heard that she had lost her job, but she didn't know which one. Also, bottles of prescription pills had appeared above the bathroom sink. Elly read the labels but didn't recognize the names. *Was Jodi still in the bath?* Elly thought. *What if she had fallen asleep? She might drown.*

Something about the situation, something about that note on the door, something about the general silence of the house drove Elly out of bed. She reluctantly exited her room and stood out in the hallway. She approached the bathroom door and took a breath. She prepared to knock.

Suddenly the doorknob turned. To avoid an awkward run-in, Elly quickly bounded into the kitchenette. She stood there on the edge of darkness and watched as the door to the bathroom came open and then humid light seeped into the hall. Jodi stepped forward. She was naked. She stood within the doorway, her arm against the wall.

Elly wanted to apologize. She wanted to make her presence known, but something wasn't right. Jodi tried to walk, but she was leaning heavily against the wall. Her buttocks shook in a clumsy way, as if the muscle of her thighs wouldn't engage.

Jodi made it to her bedroom door. She opened the door, and then collapsed onto the carpet. Elly pulled out her phone and dialled 911. While talking to the operator, she returned to watch as Jodi dragged herself across the floor towards her bed. Having noticed now that Elly was standing in the doorway, Jodi tried to pull a blanket over her body.

Jodi lit a cigarette, lying in bed. I think I'm going to need to see a doctor, she said, waving her arm in the air.

She had an awkward gash that ran several inches down the length of her forearm. It looked fake, Crayola-coloured, Elly thought.

Back in the bathroom, a wineglass had been shattered by the tub. There was an open bottle of cherry-flavoured vodka in the sink and bottles of Jodi's pills were scattered. The water in the bathtub was a rosy pink. Elly, still on the phone with a dispatch worker, was supposed to be describing the scene, but found herself distracted by the smell. The room smelled of both a body and the earth. Like excrement and sex, vomit, sweat and morning breath rolled into one.

Jodi was stuffing the butt of a cigarette into an overflowing ashtray by her bed. She was lighting another one when Elly returned.

What do you think of it? Jodi asked.

Elly shook her head. It doesn't matter what I think. The ambulance is coming.

Oh, come on, Jodi persisted. Her words were slurred. Her tongue was thick.

Listen, you're going to the hospital. You're probably going to be there for a number of days. Do you want me to pack you anything?

Looking almost disappointed, Jodi pointed at a knapsack on the floor. First, she said, my blue robe.

Your blue rope?

My *robe*. Jodi pointed again.

Elly packed a pair of slippers and some books. Jodi wanted her to pack a carton of cigarettes, indicating with a wave that Elly should look around the table in the middle of the room. There were at least a dozen packs, some fallen to the floor, but each was empty.

All gone? Jodi asked. What a shame.

Elly moved around the room, packing anything she thought might be useful. Whenever Jodi was quiet too long, Elly said something to try to keep her talking. Just a moment ago, the dispatch worker had insisted that Jodi not be allowed to sleep, but Jodi was talking less and less. She seemed to be growing tired, slipping off. Jodi hummed to get her attention, and Elly saw that she'd extended her arm. The ash on her cigarette was ready to fall, but she didn't have the strength to reach the ashtray.

Paramedics arrived, and then the police. Franny and Zooey started barking as so many bodies made their way into the room. Elly dragged the dogs, still in their kennels, out of the room and into her own bedroom. She set their cages face to face so that each dog would have something to look at. Next, Elly talked to an officer who questioned her at length about what had happened, what she had seen, about Jodi, and then more generally about the house. This basement, was it a detached suite? But it had a separate entrance though, correct? And how many others were living upstairs? And where was everybody tonight?

How long have you known Miss Dunn? the officer asked. And do you know why she would do this to herself?

Elly didn't know. There had been indications of a vague distress and Elly'd been a witness to its development, but this was just the nature of living with strangers. Your life becomes theirs, and theirs yours in a way, but there is no real understanding.

As the paramedics led Jodi out of her room, one on either side of her holding her up, her feet hardly touched the floor. Elly sat on the stairs. She thought Jodi looked like an old woman, one who had just tried something daring and impossible. She looked frail, but wild with her orange hair. Then Jodi looked up, and the impression faded.

Seeing Elly, Jodi smiled widely. You'll come visit me in the hospital, right?

The next day, Elly woke up alone. It was grey, and maybe ten in the morning. For a while after getting out of bed, she stood looking out of her bedroom window. Outside there was a mist so heavy, so thick, it collected on the trees and fell like rain.

She thought of Jodi. She also thought of Tom. She thought of Sam while standing there, looking on the world outside. Now, with only her fingertips, she reached one more time to touch the glass. Before pushing, she tried to believe that this time the window would swing open wide.

YOU'RE GETTING OLDER

Marcelo had spent the evening drinking with friends. Now it was after midnight and he was biking home to be with his girlfriend. He was biking without wearing his mittens, even though the cold bit into his hands. He had been smoking and he wanted to air the smell of cigarettes from his fingers, and for the same reason, he was breathing deeply with his mouth open wide in order to freshen his breath. Like many, his girlfriend Larissa didn't much like the smell of cigarettes and beer in her bed.

Marcelo wasn't in any hurry, so was biking slowly, weaving down the middle of the street. He stopped when he heard a lady call out to him. Oh, young man! Can you help me, please?

The lady was standing on the sidewalk and emerged from the shadow of a tree. She came into the street taking the small, hurried steps of someone aged and full of worry.

I can help you, said Marcelo. What do you need?

You have to come with me, said the lady.

Marcelo turned his bike around and followed her past several houses up the street. The lady had a dishevelled look, and the exaggerated pleading in her voice had made him wary. Marcelo congratulated himself on his ability to maintain a degree of skepticism, despite his otherwise natural desire to be of help. Also, it felt good to have affected a certain level-headedness when in truth he was really somewhat drunk.

There's an old woman on the floor, the lady said.

Marcelo followed the lady to her building and carried his bike up the few stairs to her landing. Her apartment was just off the street. The lady opened the door, but bent over in the doorway in order to arrange things on the floor. Marcelo could hear groaning coming from within and he wanted to get inside, but the lady was squarely in the way. He heard a clinking of empty bottles as she moved some plastic grocery bags. The lady tried to arrange these decently, along with an unsorted pile of shoes. Marcelo didn't care about the decency of the lady's entryway, though. He felt like telling her that she was wasting time, to stop cleaning the place on his account.

Finally, the lady turned and let him in. She led him through the living room, down the hall, and then stopped at a bedroom door. The door was open and Marcelo could see the two bare legs of a woman on the floor. He extended himself into the room and saw that this old woman must have fallen from her bed. She was lying on her back, wearing a nightgown that had fallen open to expose her yellowed underwear. The woman was groaning, making a continuous, guttural noise. Marcelo stood above her, but the woman's eyes remained fixed. She was looking up at the ceiling, but her eyes were focused impossibly far away.

There were twin beds in the room, each with a matching floral comforter. The woman had fallen off the far side of one bed, so she lay in the narrow space between the bed frame and the wall.

She does this all the time, said the lady, as if to lay the blame for this whole incident on the woman, who must have been some kind of roommate to her. Even as she said it though, the lady exhibited a kind of nervous helplessness.

Marcelo thought the woman must have had a kind of stroke. Did you call an ambulance? he asked. Have you got a phone somewhere?

Together, they moved into the living room. There was a chair beneath the window, and a table. On the table was an old rotary phone. On every other surface and in every corner of the room were piles of clutter—books, garments, paper cups, knick-knacks and old magazines.

To the 911 operator, Marcelo heard the lady saying, She'll be eighty-two next spring. Oh goodness, I don't know, I really don't know…

Back in the bedroom the old woman was grabbing at the side of the bed, feebly trying to lift herself. Marcelo kneeled beside her. She was able to get her shoulders off the floor, to lift them just a couple inches, but her head hung back and her eyes stayed fixed as if looking up into the sky. Marcelo touched her forearm. The woman recoiled and the groaning stopped.

She looked at him and hissed, Your hands are like ice. Then just as suddenly, the groaning started up again.

Marcelo apologized. He made a big show of rubbing his hands together. He urged her to remain on the floor until the paramedics came. He put a pillow under her head.

Is there anything else I can do to make you more comfortable? he asked. He spoke a half-octave higher than normal, in the servile manner of a person waiting tables.

You could put me in that chair, the woman instructed.

She's stubborn, said the lady who, having returned from her phone call, was now standing again at the bedroom door. She has no patience and she can't accept directives.

Marcelo offered to cover the woman with a blanket. It would be good for her, he figured, but also he wanted to put some barrier between himself and the intimacy of her body.

Put me in that chair, the woman insisted.

Again, she was trying to pull herself up from the floor. It seemed the only way for Marcelo and the lady to try to calm her, so against all better judgement, they prepared to lift her into the chair. First they stood in front of her and pulling on her arms, tried to position her onto her feet, but the woman had no strength in her legs. Her body was flabby and loose like an under-inflated water balloon, and was impossible to grip. They tried again, but this time Marcelo went around and kneeled behind her. He sat her up and she leaned into him and in this way, he was able to lift her in stages.

But when the crucial moment came to slip the woman into the chair, Marcelo felt her falling from his arms. He knew in an instant that the only way to hold her would be to reach below and take her by the back of her thighs. He saw that her legs were doughy and pale. He hesitated, but she continued to slip. He knew he had to act. Reaching as close to her knees as was possible, he managed to secure her and thus get her into the chair. As soon as that was done, the old lady started edging him out.

Oh, thank you, she said. Thank you, thank you so much. She waved her arms up dramatically and pressed him to leave the room. In the hallway, she handed him a five-dollar bill. I know it isn't much, the lady said.

Marcelo tried to decline the money, but the lady insisted he take it. She went to tuck it into his pocket, but Marcelo dodged her. Finally, she stuffed it into the collar of his jacket. He could feel the paper rub against his neck.

Are you sure you don't want me to stay a little longer? Marcelo offered.

Oh, no. You've been so kind, but no.

The lady ushered him out through the living room. Marcelo took the fiver from his collar and pressed it into some clutter on a mantle as he passed.

What was that? the lady snapped. What did you do? She looked at the mantle, and when she saw the bill, she grabbed it and lurched at him. You have to take this, she said, almost pleading, and stuffed it one more time into the collar of his jacket.

Before she closed the door, Marcelo offered again to stay, at least until the ambulance arrived.

She does this all the time, the lady said. In fact, I'm going to cancel that call. There's no need anymore for them to come, don't you think? Oh, if you could only imagine all the trouble, all the bother, everything I have to— The lady had worked herself into a kind of excited fit.

You should try to calm down. You shouldn't cancel the call. She'll be fine.

But what if she isn't? he said, then regretted it immediately.

The lady's face hardened. She closed the door and secured the bolt.

Marcelo stood on the landing with his bike. For a moment he considered putting the five-dollar bill into the mailbox, or sticking it between the weather stripping and the door, but he didn't see any mailbox or any obvious place to leave it, so he stuck the thing into his pocket.

While biking the rest of the way home, Marcelo wondered about several things. It bothered him that the woman had been so set on getting up and into the chair when it was so clearly in her best interest to remain on the floor. It bothered him, yet he thought he could understand her willfulness. What he could not understand was why the old lady had wasted time to tidy up her entryway before she'd let him into the apartment. And why hadn't she wanted him to stay a little longer, in case things with the woman got worse? Why had he been in that apartment at all? Only to lift a woman into a chair? What kind of a deed was that? Had the situation really been much improved? Those damned women, Marcelo thought. They didn't want to see any improvement. They just wanted to maintain their status quo. And if the one was going to die, the other would let it happen, simply trying maintain things as they'd always been. Marcelo decided that in the end, it's up to people how they want to live and die. And after he decided that, he quit thinking about it.

At home, he said to Larissa, Something really strange just happened.

Was there a man downstairs? Did he try to get in? Apparently, Larissa had her own strange story to tell. Some guy, she explained, called my phone and wanted me to let him into the building. I told him I wasn't comfortable with that, that maybe he should call the landlady.

'Call the landlady?' the guy said. 'It's after midnight!'

He told me that my number was like a contact number for the building, but obviously that isn't right. I think maybe he was at the wrong building? Because he kept saying, 'Unit 45.' I told him there were only three apartments here, and that we were new tenants. He said, 'Tenants?' Anyway, I couldn't understand him. He couldn't understand me. But for a long time he just wouldn't let me off the phone.

Marcelo took off all his clothes and put them into the laundry basket. He took a shower to forget the woman's smell. Afterward, he and Larissa sat on the bed and talked for several hours. Larissa had spent the night looking into a master's program on the other side of the country. She wasn't sure what to do about it, whether or not she wanted to apply. She and Marcelo had only recently moved here, and had barely settled in. Neither of them had lined up any work yet and already their savings were dwindling.

Before turning out the light, Larissa sighed, What are we going to do with our lives?

The next day, Marcelo awoke after Larissa had gone out. He made himself a cup of tea and took a walk around the neighbourhood. He walked to a nearby restaurant where he had thought of applying for work, but by the time he reached the place he'd already lost interest in the idea. It was cold out, so he turned back home.

That afternoon, he looked into the option of attending a trade school. Part of him wanted to get something going beyond restaurant work and simple labour jobs. He thought he wouldn't mind working with wood down the road, but he couldn't find any suitable courses. Ultimately, he wasn't sure if he was keen. Marcelo didn't like to look at the big picture. It was hard for him to imagine ever wanting to choose a single career. There was a part of him still that wanted to keep working at a dead-end job, to work for another couple of years without any ambition, and to enjoy the time as it slipped away.

Marcelo's mother called to say hello, and he made the mistake of sharing his confusion with her. She only reminded him of all the barriers that lay ahead in life for a person who doesn't pursue financial security early on.

You're getting older, his mother said.

Marcelo looked at the five-dollar bill the lady had given him. He briefly considered going out to buy a lottery ticket with the money, thinking it would be a strangely appropriate bill to expend in order to win ten thousand dollars. But really, he knew it wasn't any more likely to buy a winning lottery ticket than another bill, regardless of the circumstances by which he'd acquired it. He decided to spend it the same as he would any money, and he put it in his wallet.

Later, his friend Dave called.

What did you do today? Dave asked.

Well, Marcelo said, Larissa was talking about doing her master's last night and she was worrying about life which got me worrying too. So I've been sitting here looking for jobs and researching schools, but I feel like I really have no interest in any of it.

Sounds like you could use a drink, said Dave.

That night, Marcelo and Dave had dinner together. Dave cooked a simple pasta. They shared a bottle of wine as they ate. Afterward, they decided to go out for beers and shoot some pool.

It was a Thursday night and the bar they chose wasn't busy. Still, they had to wait some time for the pool table, but they were happy enough just sitting and drinking their beers. When they finally did get a table, they played a game against two French-Canadians. One was old and drunk, the other young and drunk with a black eye and a row of broken teeth. Both were awfully drunk to be playing pool.

Soon enough, Marcelo and Dave were drunk as well. They smoked some of Dave's cigarettes outside the bar. They talked about books and the night wore on. The small crowd inside the bar thinned out. The only waitress in the place sang karaoke when she wasn't serving drinks. And before leaving, without even having noticed, Marcelo used the five-dollar bill crammed in his wallet to pay for yet another round.

ABOUT FRANKLIN

1.

The first time I ever met Franklin was when he came to the apartment one night. He came over to see Annie of course, who was my roommate, also my best friend and the only person I really thought I cared about. She and I shared this little place near the university with two bedrooms, a small balcony and a piano in the living room. The piano was an object of luxury, an instrument neither of us knew how to play. Annie, because she had never learned, and although I had taken lessons as a girl, I had forgotten everything.

That night started the same as any other. Annie and I were in her bedroom. She was sitting on the bed while I was lying on the floor. Lately we'd been spending practically every night of the week this way, just passing the time, doing nothing of any consequence—sometimes reading poetry aloud from magazines, or talking, drawing, taking pictures, or making little works of art. We were always in Annie's bedroom because there was a warmth to the place. It was like a manifestation of her personality. Annie's room had a charming, cozy, sedate atmosphere. I remember it retrospectively as if it were lit in a rose-coloured light. But as I was saying, we were doing almost nothing that night when all of a sudden we heard a noise at the window. It was a small but definitive sound, as if of something sporadically hitting the glass. Annie went to investigate. She stuck her head out the window and I heard her speak to someone. She explained it was Franklin, standing below.

I try to remember when the first time was that Annie spoke to me about Franklin. It must have been something said in passing, something practically whispered, some insignificant detail thrown into an unremarkable anecdote. Then over a course of days, of maybe weeks, his name must have come up again, but always in a casual way. Always: Oh and of course Franklin was there. Or: I bumped into Franklin on my way out the door. Or still: Then Franklin sneezed so loud that people ten rows ahead of us turned around to see. It was all very subtle, very under the radar. Though, if you asked Annie, I'm sure she'd remember it differently. Probably she would tell you that I was always distracted, forgetful, that I never could grasp all the details of this, nor of anything else for that matter. Still the impression remains, that when I finally realized she was seeing this boy, that she and he had become *involved*, I was left with a feeling that Annie had been, for some reason, keeping me in the dark. Finally, I asked her once and for all who this Franklin guy was, but she only rolled her eyes.

Now here was Franklin standing three storeys down in the parking lot, throwing pebbles up into the night. But why pebbles? I wanted to ask. After all, wasn't there a working inter-com? Was he trying to be romantic?

Looking back I can say that the answer is no, Franklin wasn't trying to be anything. I didn't know it yet, but Franklin did a lot of things differently, and it was not because he wanted to appear different, not because he tried to be different. Sometimes you have to wonder about a person, how would they behave if they could be left alone. I mean, if they could be utterly, completely alone, what would they do with themselves? And how would they do what they did? I think that in such a case, Franklin would do things more or less as he had always done. He would stand in front of empty buildings throwing pebbles up at bed-room windows belonging to no one.

Annie went downstairs to let Franklin into the building. I went into the kitchen to fill a glass with water from the tap. I had a vague feeling of apprehension, and I didn't know wheth-er it was nervousness about the fact that soon I'd be meeting someone, or whether I was in some way upset about a stranger's intrusion into our night. Maybe I was only bewildered, because after all it still felt strange to me that Annie could be dating someone. I had simply never considered her as a romantic or a sexual being. She was so friendly and had so many friends. She was always making friends with people everywhere she went. Honestly, I thought it had to be awkward to have sex with any-one, and Annie seemed only too natural, too comfortable with nearly everyone she met.

I heard them come in the door. I was on my way down the hall when Franklin and I crossed paths. He hardly acknow-ledged me. It was as if we were in a hotel, each on our way to our separate rooms. And the hall was only dimly lit, so I didn't get a good look at him. I could see that he was older than Annie and me by at least a few years. He was thin, not very tall, and had a mop of dark, curly hair. He wore a ragged, knitted sweater which billowed unbuttoned away from his body, so to avoid running into him I found myself practically pressed up against the wall. I almost spilled my water, in fact. Then Annie came gliding in after him. Without a word she guided Franklin into her bedroom and closed the door. I was left standing for a moment in the hall. I thought I could hear them laughing, but what did I know? Maybe they were crying, I thought. Or maybe they were fucking already.

After a while I went into my own room. I was supposed to be studying for a mid-term exam I would write in the morning anyway. The exam was for a literary survey course called, "An Introduction to the Novel." I went to my desk and sat with the novel we had been reading most recently, *A Hundred Years of Solitude* by Gabriel García Márquez. Beyond holding the book though, I didn't really know what to do with it. I didn't know how to study properly. I opened the book, turned a few pages, then somehow an hour went by, and when Annie came into the room she found me running my finger over the surface of the water in my drinking glass. She knocked at the door, even though it was open, and told me that she and Franklin were going for a walk.

Do you want to come along? she asked.

Maybe, I said. Where are you going?

She told me they were going to take a walk to the end of the street and get high. Of course I wanted to go, but I'd also promised myself that I'd try not to smoke anything tonight. If I wasn't going to be studying, the very least I could do was to try to keep a clear head for the morning. Back then I was a real pushover when it came to smoking pot. If somebody offered it to me, I couldn't refuse, not once the thought had entered my head. Sometimes if I only caught the scent of it, say as I was walking on my way to a class—and it could be the middle of the afternoon, but if there was a hint of marijuana in the air—it made me want to drop everything, to drop off the face of the Earth and get thoroughly, miserably, blissfully stoned. Because for me the high was all in the smell. The high was in the taste of it on my mouth. I told Annie that yes, I wanted to come.

I was introduced to Franklin at the door. He was surprisingly formal about it. As he shook my hand—and I think he even made a slight bow—he said, Charlie. It's really great to meet you. Annie's told me so many things.

I thought I ought to say something equally kind, but I didn't know what. After a moment, my hand still in his, I blurted out, Franklin. It's really great to meet you too. Annie's told me so many things.

Annie snorted. Oh jeez, she said.

We left the apartment and passed quietly down the carpeted hallways, but it was only once we had left the building I realized that Franklin wasn't wearing shoes. At first I thought maybe he'd forgotten them, either upstairs or at home, so I asked. Franklin chuckled and told me that he hadn't forgotten them.

Annie said, Franklin isn't wearing shoes, as if that was any kind of explanation.

Is it because you're trying to toughen up the soles of your feet? I asked.

Actually, there is no real reason, Franklin said. I stopped wearing shoes about a month ago just to see what it would be like, and I'm not wearing them now because I want to see how long this will go on. I suppose in a way I'm waiting for something to tell me when to stop.

Or to tell you when to start, I said.

Franklin chuckled again. Yeah, he said, that's right.

We slowly made our way down the street to where it dead-ended into a cluster of trees. It was only March, but it had been unseasonably warm recently, and some of the buds on those branches had already burst. It was a dark night, and while walking we didn't say anything more, only every so often Franklin quietly cooed, sounding just like a pigeon.

After smoking we spent a while talking. We talked about Franklin, about Annie, about the two of them together. Franklin asked me about myself. He wanted to know what I was studying, and did I like it, and if not, where did my interests lie. I don't remember how it came about, but I think at some point we talked about the poet Pablo Neruda. Had I ever read any Neruda? And what did I think of his works? I remember Annie had one of his books, a slender volume of his poetry. So when I think about Pablo Neruda today, I think about Annie's hands. I think about her hands holding onto that book, her little hands, and then about her little feet, and I think of how in some ways she always was so small and delicate. When I think about Annie today, I think here is someone who deserves to be loved. When I think about Pablo Neruda I see only anger and a hard masculinity. I see a brutal aggressivity lurking there beneath his most sensitive lines. When I think about Pablo Neruda, I think here is the spirit of something willing to beat a woman into the dust. But then what did I know? And what was important? Standing there at the end of the street, what mattered was that we were getting along. Of course, Annie was thrilled to see her new boyfriend and her best friend hitting it off. Franklin mentioned that he'd be leaving soon to go travelling through Europe. Annie was hoping to join him there sometime later in the spring. Franklin said I shouldn't expect to see him again since he would be leaving so soon. And thanks to a streetlight, I had managed to get a good look at his face. He had a high brow, clever eyes and a slightly hooked nose. He had the features of a hawk, I thought. And actually, that's one way to think of him— as a hawk who coos like a pigeon, or as a man who doesn't wear shoes. And I mean that figuratively, whether or not he really is wearing shoes.

Two weeks later Franklin was gone and although I knew it didn't make sense, I felt as if he'd left me behind. I was sad to see him go, but it was something more than that. It didn't often happen that I met someone I could relate with as easily as I related with him. Franklin was unique, and I had felt a kind of chemistry between us, so it was sad to see him slip away, headed in another direction, headed off and out of my life. As for Annie, who in this situation really had been left behind, if she was hurt, she didn't show it. She was just her usually kind, effusive self.

One night she dragged me to a party hosted by one of Franklin's friends. As it happened, most of Franklin's friends had by now become Annie's friends as well. The party was at a girl named Julia's house. Actually, it was at her parents' house which was in one of those wealthy, labyrinthine-like neighbourhoods built against the shore. So many of Franklin's friends seemed still to be living with their parents, I'd noticed. I thought it must be because they had grown up in this city, unlike Annie and I who were strangers here and still sometimes felt lost.

On the night of the party we rode our bicycles down those long and winding roads. We circled traffic roundabouts, passing under massive cedar trees. It was incomprehensible to me that

Annie should know where we were going, but she led the way and I followed. It was an easy ride downhill all the way toward the sea, and after twenty minutes, we arrived at the house.

We parked our bikes against the garage and walked around the side of the house. In the backyard there were a dozen people or so, some standing over a barbecue, some smoking cigarettes in the dark. I thought it must be a new moon since I could hardly see anyone's face. Only an errant feature here or there displayed, such as a pair of lips or half a nose glimpsed in the cherry-glow of a cigarette. Annie and I tried mingling. We joined into conversations. But all the while it was as if people were speaking in a foreign tongue. We felt disoriented, overwhelmed, and by the time we finally made it into the house, we didn't know who we'd been talking to or what had been said, so we worried we had been somehow compromised. It was as if we had suffered a memory lapse, as if we had given something away without keeping track of what it was and of who it had been given to. Maybe it wouldn't have mattered if we hadn't already smoked so much pot, but as it was, we thought we needed safety so we found the kitchen and made a kind of mental fortress there. What I mean is that we set up camp. The kitchen was bright and clean. We took out the bottle of wine we'd brought and planted it like a flag on the granite counter. Then we took turns drinking, swigging straight out of the bottle. We found that the more we drank, the better we felt, and soon we were feeling so good we had even started laughing at ourselves. That's how Julia found us, standing in the kitchen and laughing. She seemed delighted to have found us at all.

I'm so glad you came, she said and gave Annie a hug. Then she turned to me and introduced herself. She gave me a hug too saying, It's really great to meet you.

Julia, it's so great to meet you too. Annie's told me so many things.

Julia smiled, but she looked confused.

Annie said, Pay no attention to her. She's drunk and stoned.

I smiled and shrugged.

Julia laughed. Then she turned more deliberately to Annie. I didn't see you come in, she said. Oh, and I love your sweater, by the way. Did you get that second hand?

Here she laid her own hand onto Annie's sleeve as if she hadn't ever felt knitwear before, and the next thing I knew, they were talking at length about a person I'd never met. I left them and wandered off to inspect another part of the house.

It was obvious Julia's family had money. Their house was large and tidy—well taken care of, but in an impersonal way. I spent some time on the staircase looking at her family photographs. Then I went into the bathroom and opened the cupboards to see what was hidden inside.

I heard music coming from the living room. In there I saw that all the furniture had been pushed against the wall, and in the middle of the room people were dancing, some singly, others in pairs. I felt embarrassed to have stumbled into this scene, but I couldn't turn around and leave. It was like I was being watched. And was I being watched, I wondered. I made my way deeper into the room, skirting the dance floor and finding a place on the couch. It wasn't long before a boy sat next to me. At first he offered me a gin drink, which I accepted, but then we couldn't find any glasses. Instead, he let me pull on his flask, which was something I had only ever seen done in movies. I told him as much, and he took it as a compliment. We spent the next twenty minutes talking, and although the boy kept saying he wanted to know all about me, he talked mostly of himself. He had nothing very interesting to say. He kept insisting he had never heard of Franklin Turner, and I kept insisting he had.

It's likely that you wouldn't remember him. Probably to most people he isn't remarkable, I said.

By now the boy seemed to be losing interest, but he asked me if I wanted to dance.

I told him I didn't know how, but he said, It's easy, I can show you. All you have to do is move your body.

I told him I didn't want to learn, that my head was already full of so many different things, and that to learn anything at this point would mean I'd need to sacrifice something else.

Are you being serious? he asked

Deadly serious, I said. I'm just not sure it's the right thing to do, to make such a sacrifice tonight.

Do you want to get out of here? he asked.

God yes, I said, and I stood up to go, but then so did the boy. Oh, I said, now I see what you mean. But that would mean learning something new.

The boy asked me if I was a virgin. I told him it was awfully rude of him to ask, and finally broke away from the boy and the living room. Back in the kitchen I found Annie still talking with Julia. I came up next to them and instinctively reached for our bottle of wine. At that moment I felt just such a terrific thirst for a mouthful of wine, but our bottle was empty. There were others though, other bottles, several of them lined up on the counter. There were whites and reds and bottles of booze, so I took a red and uncorked it.

Just as I was raising the bottle to my lips, a girl came in, saw what I was doing and screamed, Is that my fucking Chianti?

I was so startled that I dropped the thing. It landed without breaking, but the force of its impact against the floor sent a streamer of wine up into the air, which hung for a moment before raining down over everyone and everything. There was a long silence during which Annie, Julia and the girl all looked to me, as if for an explanation.

I sighed. You know, I see this primarily as an issue of private ownership.

Nobody said anything, so I cooed like a pigeon. Annie laughed so hard that she fired a mouthful of water out of her nose.

Afterward I offered to tidy up, but Julia brushed me off. I apologized instead, both to the hostess and to the girl. Annie apologized once more to Julia on my behalf and we excused ourselves, went out the back, through the yard and around the house again. It was slow going as we rode our bicycles home. It was uphill all the way.

Annie left for Europe in May. She would be gone for ten weeks, and in that time she would keep in touch by writing emails regularly. She would write them as if they were letters, making them long and sentimental, the first coming out of Amsterdam. Annie wrote that she had landed the day before and that Franklin had come to meet her at the train station. *He looked good,* she wrote. He seemed happy. He seemed genuinely glad that she was there. Later that afternoon, after getting acquainted with the city together, they had gone and eaten magic mushrooms. *And that day was like a blossom,* Annie wrote, *like an opening in the very heart of hearts, with all of life expanding outwards, past and future outwards both, growing from a singular point. Simple objects resonated,* she wrote, *with significance, and no city ever looked so good.* In the evening she and Franklin had had a dispute with the owner of a hotel. They had already planned to stay the night and had reserved a room at a given rate, but now the owner was demanding more money. Franklin made a big scene of it, yelling at the man and even kicking the desk, but really it was only a joke. Together they stormed out of the hotel, laughing, hollering, slamming the door. They slept that night in a public park, lying in the grass under the trees.

Sometime later Annie wrote me an email from Greece saying she and Franklin had fallen in love. Now every night before going to sleep they took turns reading to each other. They were reading out of Rainer Maria Rilke's *Letters to a Young Poet. Have you ever read Rilke?* she wrote. *It really is something else. It feels like nourishment, like something fulfilling, exquisite and sensual. It's like a slice of melon, perfectly ripe.* Annie even went on to quote some lines they'd been reading the night before: *It is good to love, because love is difficult. For one human being to love another human being, that is perhaps the most difficult task that has been entrusted to us, the ultimate task, the final test and proof, the work for which all other work is merely preparation.*

Following her suggestion, I did try reading that book, but I didn't get far. Something about it bothered me, annoyed me, made me angry. Because here was Rilke, a formidable poet, writing letters to a younger one, saying how, for instance, we are alone in the deepest, most important things, saying how one person never can know the life of another one, and should therefore never try to guide or to counsel. While on the other hand here was Rilke, an older poet, playing mentor and teacher, playing wisdom itself, laying his own conception of life heavy-handedly onto the younger one. It was just so very hypocritical, besides the fact that I didn't care at all for the way he wrote. It annoyed me that with Rilke everything needed be so deep and meaningful. So potent, grave and so full of ache. I put that book aside, but then a few weeks went by and I thought I might try and give it another shot, if only for the sake of Annie. This time *Letters* made me feel so sick and mad that I ended up tearing the book in half. I mean, without thinking, taking it in my hands and tearing it along the spine, and more or less instantly any feeling of sickness and anger was gone. But now I had these two halves of a book, so I did what anyone would do and put them on a shelf, after which I thought about Annie. I thought about her and her being in love. I thought that maybe when it came to this book I had overreacted in a way. I had been hard on Rilke, and by extension, had been hard on my friend. But that was as much as I thought before I had to turn my attention to other things. Right at that moment, my own life was in the midst of being flipped and turned around. With Annie in Europe, I hadn't been able to afford to keep the apartment, and so had to pack up my things. I took a few boxes that Annie had left behind and brought them to a friend's for storage. But there was nowhere to store the piano.

The piano belonged to Annie, so I asked her what she wanted done with it. At first I didn't get any response, so I tried calling her parents. I thought that maybe because it had been a gift, they might have some idea of what I should do. I got her mother on the phone, but all she could say was that I ought to talk to Annie about it. I tried writing to Annie again, and this time she wrote me back, but still she forgot to say anything about the piano. Finally, it was almost the day when I had to leave, and still I didn't know what to do. At the last moment I arranged to have the piano sold and used the money to pay off the last of our bills. I boarded a Greyhound bus and rode it inland overnight, over the mountains and into the flatland town where my mother lived.

It had been a year since I'd left this town, and although my coming back was only meant to be temporary, it felt like I had failed at something. If I had managed to do better, I thought, if I had done things somehow differently, then I wouldn't need to spend the summer at home.

The town was smaller than I had remembered it. My mother's house was smaller too. I felt like Alice in Wonderland when she winds up stuck in the rabbit's house, afraid that if I moved too suddenly my limbs might burst out the windows or the door. At night I would walk through the house, moving slowly from room to room. I would stop along the way to study objects, each item so familiar, but also like something I remembered from a dream.

Most nights I would need to leave the house. At one or two o'clock in the morning I would go out through the patio door, quietly easing it shut behind me, always careful not to wake up my mom. I didn't have any reason to be sneaking out, I just didn't want to explain myself, to answer questions about where I was going or what I was doing and why whatever I was doing needed to be done at such an unusual hour.

On those nights I would walk to the river, find a bench to sit on and roll a joint. I would drink a cup of tea at the coffee shop on the highway, which was open all night. Sometimes I would wander streets at random, going up and down, past houses, parks and the landmarks of my youth. Every place I went was quiet. The town was calm, vacant, so I felt as if I were walking on a stage. Everywhere was lit artificially, the streetlights bearing onto summer leaves, the shadows cast like puddles that I went stepping in and out of.

Pretty soon the days began to resemble one another. I realized I didn't have any friends. Most of the people I'd known here had by now left and hadn't returned, and all those who remained had become disconnected socially. That, at least, was my impression of things. But the truth is I didn't really make any effort. I wasn't looking to find anyone. After all, sleeping all day and walking through town every night stoned wasn't a life that I wanted to share with anyone. I wasn't looking for company. I was more or less killing time.

The problem was of writing to Annie. It was a problem because multiple times every week she would send me a description of where she had been, and her emails were full of feeling and inspiration. But what could I offer her in return? What could I give to her? What did I have?

One night I thought I must be losing my mind, being certain I heard the wind calling out my name. At the time, I was near the high school, passing through the fields out back when I heard it. I turned this way and that, looked all around, but there was no one there. I strained my ears and thought, Oh shit, because there it was again. After what felt like a long time of standing like a duck in the field, I spotted someone in the distance. Whoever it was was waving their arms in the air, trying to get my attention. This person was on the bleachers by the baseball diamond, and as I started in that direction, he started toward me. Only when we were close did I realize it was Paul, someone I had known in high school.

First he asked what I was doing out here. I said that I could ask him the same thing. Instead of answering, Paul started to laugh.

I've seen you lately out and about. At first I wasn't sure it was you, but nobody else I know ever walked like that, said Paul.

Walked like that? What is that supposed to mean? I asked.

Paul just laughed again.

Paul and I dated, but our relationship had been a mistake. We weren't friends before we dated, so it was never clear if we even liked each other that much. We used to argue all the time about stupid things, and we never spent any time alone. I felt like he was dragging me out just to parade me in front of his friends, though not because he thought I was beautiful or pretty, or even nice, but to show them that here was a girl who would follow him, who would go wherever he wanted to go and do what he wanted to do. Since then though, something had changed in him. Something had softened. He looked tired, but he was smiling.

We left the field behind the school and wound up walking together, wandering until we found a picnic table in a park where we sat and rolled a joint. After smoking, Paul told me a little about his life. He said he had started working in his uncle's automotive shop. He was only an apprentice so he did a lot of menial work, things like rotating tires and changing oil, filters and fluids. He told me that at night he didn't get much sleep. When he got home from work he'd typically smoke a bowl and have something to eat, then he'd lie on the couch for a while and try not to think about anything.

I asked, What do you wind up thinking about?

I think about all fucking kinds of things, Paul replied.

So it doesn't work? I asked.

What doesn't work? It's all the same. Nothing, everything. The problem is that I can't help going out at night, driving all around, moving in circles with circular people. Everybody's always getting drunk and high, and the next thing I know it's five in the morning and the birds are out making a racket. I'm lying in bed, but I can't get to sleep. That's when I start to feel sick. I panic and I wonder how I'm going to do it again and again and again. I mean, if I really can't sleep, what'll I do tomorrow, and then tomorrow after that? How can I get through it? Where's the end of it? How can I function? It's pretty miserable, and that is by far the worst part of my day.

What's the best part of your day? I asked.

The best is when I do get to sleep, when for an hour or two I get to be totally wiped off the face of the Earth. I don't dream about anything. I don't see anything, hear anything. I don't think. I don't even feel anything.

I laughed. I'm sorry, I said. I know I'm not supposed to laugh.

It's fine, said Paul. I get it.

We stayed in the park until Paul said he had to go. I went home but was too stoned to sleep. For a while I lay in bed and, while watching the daylight grow at the window, thought about the difference between nothing and everything.

When the sun came up, I was still awake and finally felt like I might have something to say, something worthwhile to write about, so I got out of bed and went straight to the computer room, but by the time I turned the computer on, waited while it booted and opened my email, I had lost whatever it was. I had wanted to write something about Paul, to tell Annie what it had been like running into him, and what it had been like to have dated him, and what it had been like to have grown up in this place, and what it was like to be back. But now, I figured, what was the point? I challenged myself for a moment to vividly remember something of my childhood, to remember really anything, but it all felt jumbled and blurred. *What was any person's history worth*, I thought, *if poorly depicted and poorly defined?*

Annie had now returned from Europe, but instead of going back to the city, she had taken a job at a fishing resort located someplace north, up the coast. She told me it was isolated, lonely, remote, by which she meant to say it was beautiful. Her job consisted of helping the mostly wealthy visitors of the resort as they entered their boats in the morning. She loaded their tackle and coolers, their rods and reels. Her shift began at five in the morning and she would push them off into the mists. Annie described herself as standing on the docks in her Cowichan sweater, wrapped up and bundled against the cold. Later, the sun would rise over the bay and dispel the mists, shortly after which the boats would start to make their ways back in. Annie would catch their ropes, tie their knots, help the boaters and their gear ashore. Then, once everyone was off the water, Annie's shift was over. She was usually off in time to catch brunch at the bistro, she explained, and for the rest of the day she was free.

I feel happy, Annie wrote. *I've been reading lots and writing some too. I've met all kinds of people. Some are guests who have come and gone, others stay longer, mostly other staff members.*

In one of her emails Annie mentioned the name of Elliot Lamn. She put it like this: *Elliot's here.*

Elliot was a cook at the resort, but he was also a student at the university. Last spring I'd seen him on campus and pointed him out to her several times. I'd said: He's over there, the one with the black hair, the round face, and when he smiles you see his teeth.

He's got teeth like a woman, Annie said. He's got little round teeth like a woman.

I told her I was in love with him.

For a while I was seeing him everywhere, all over campus, wherever I looked. He'd be standing in front of the library or sitting by the fountain reading a book. He was waiting in line at the SUB or standing at a bus stop talking with a friend. He even turned up in my Intro to Anthropology class. It was a lecture class with a large number of students. I always sat a few rows behind Elliot, off to one side, but I never spoke to him. I never even came close. It was only through a mutual friend that I learned his name.

Now Annie was writing, *Elliot's here.* Saying, *Elliot and I have become friends.* Telling me that at the end of his shift they would sometimes meet one another in the banquet hall. The place would be dark and deserted. They would lie on top of tables and talk, looking at the ceiling. Apparently this resort was near the place where Elliot had grown up. Annie wrote that his parents still lived in a cottage somewhere nearby and that he'd told her he would take her there, some weekend soon, and that they would walk in his mother's garden and spin records in his father's den. Annie wrote, *I've told him everything about you, and as you can imagine, he's very intrigued.*

According to another one of her emails, this resort and the whole of the northwest coast was a place of both beauty and of significance. Annie wrote, *You can't help feeling the weight of it. The way the hours progress, or fall, or crash like waves against the rocks. Whenever it rains here, there's a deluge and it isn't possible to be outside so everyone gathers together, all the visitors, all the staff. We sit in the bistro or the lobby bar. We eat, drink, sit and talk, play cards and other games. And then it's like worlds have collided. You realize that everyone here has found their way through wit and happenstance to this place. To be sitting here, most of us far from home… Every so often though, each of us peels ourselves away from the group. We see out the windows, through the curtain of rain. We look and see the great, grey, dismal, desperate sea and we are practically broken then, each of us. We are temporarily crushed. But always we return, we come back to the room, back to the food, the drink and the din. We come back to the voices, back to the faces, back to the others around the table.*

From my seat at the computer, I turned to look out the window, but since it was dark, I only saw a wane reflection of myself against the glass. Now it was time for me to write, but I struggled, wondering what I should say.

Dear Annie,

I figured out recently that if instead of walking in circles I decided to walk in a continuous, straight line, and that if I only kept walking indefinitely, I might make it out to the ends of the Earth. I mean, I know you really can't walk to the ends of the Earth, but what I realized is that life could be as simple as a march down the length of a singular road. You just walk until you can't anymore. You walk until you die.

As for me, I'm too scared to try it. I go out, but I stay within the limits of town. I always eventually turn around, go home and get back into bed. And then inevitably it's already morning. And the sky is already turning blue. And I can't get to sleep for the birds...

2.

For the next school year, Annie and I found a different place to rent. This place was a house, a big old house, so big in fact that it made us laugh. There was so much more space than we would ever need, more than we would ever be able to use. There were four bedrooms, a kitchen, dining and living rooms, even a basement downstairs and a sprawling yard out the back. We could have had roommates, other friends, but we decided to keep it all to ourselves. It was a kind of luxury, and one we could afford because the house was cheap. It was cheap because it was a little run down and out of the way, standing at the end of a long road full of farms and fields, all set against the edge of the woods.

I came into the city on a Saturday afternoon, but because of some confusion I wasn't able to get into the house. Annie would be in the next day, and only then would we meet the landlord, hand over our cheques and be given the keys. In the meantime, I had a duffle bag and a knapsack that I carried from the bus station onto a local bus that brought me to the end of our road. I started walking, but it was almost an hour before I finally arrived, only to find that the previous tenants were still packing up their things and loading boxes into their vehicles. I stood on the road for a while and watched, then decided that the best thing to do would be to hide my duffle bag somewhere nearby and make off in the direction of a park I knew to be close by. I hoped that there I might be able to find a place to sleep.

The park was on a piece of property along the waterfront, so for a time I sat on the beach and watched the evening slowly coming on. I lay on a log and tried to rest, but time and again I was interrupted. People came by walking dogs, couples came strolling hand in hand. Finally, before it was dark, I decided to leave. It was getting cold by the water anyway, so I decided to move, to walk back into the city, and once there, to make some plan as to what I should do.

I spent that night trying to find a place to close my eyes. At some point, I gave up and bought a tall cup of sugary coffee from a convenience store and took it to a bus shelter where I pretended to wait for a bus. From the shelter I could hear the sounds of a party not far away. I could even make out the smell of liquor and cheap beer hanging in the air. Later some guests of the party started filtering by on the sidewalk, small groups of boys and girls, most likely students like myself. Some of them tried to tell me that it was too late, that the bus wasn't running anymore. I shrugged, and so they repeated themselves. It's like, three in the morning, they said. Don't you get it? Some asked me where I was going and invited me to walk with them. I told them I wasn't going anywhere, that I was just waiting for a bus, but these people were drunk so they quickly lost interest. They walked off and left me alone.

The next day, dawn was unusually bright. By ten o'clock I had made my way back to the house, which was when Annie was supposed to arrive. Yesterday's tenants were gone, but it still didn't feel right for me to approach the place, so after pulling my duffle bag out the neighbour's hedge, I sat on the opposite curb and waited. Eventually a minivan pulled into the driveway and a short, bald man stepped out. I wondered if he had noticed me, but he didn't give any sign that he had. A few minutes later there was another minivan in the driveway. I saw Annie coming out of the driver's side and a boy I didn't recognize came out of the passenger's side, and then the three of them—Annie, the boy and the landlord—stood in a circle, shaking hands.

At first I didn't do anything. It was like I had forgotten I was meant to be part of the scene. I was tired after a sleepless night, and it was surreal to see Annie. There she was, just a hundred yards away, standing, talking, shaking hands, moving through the world with her trademark cheeriness and confidence. It occurred to me that this was more or less what she had been doing these last few months. Moving through the world and living her life, in a brilliance of mornings such as this. Suddenly I missed her so terribly that I didn't even bother with my bags, I just stood from the curb, crossed the street, climbed the driveway, and then before anybody knew what was happening, wrapped myself around her in a great big, ridiculous, needy hug. Next came the introductions, to the landlord and to the boy, who as it turned out was Annie's younger brother. He had come for the ride and to help Annie move. Tomorrow he would return the van, which belonged to their parents. For now though, her brother was grinning. Annie was laughing and asking where I had come from. I gestured vaguely towards the road. The land-lord admitted he had noticed me earlier but said he hadn't known what to make of me.

The rest of the day consisted of us being shown through-out the house. Cheques and keys were exchanged. Papers were signed. Annie, her brother and I moved a few things into the house. All of what we owned so far barely made a dent in the space. Next, we made a trip to the grocery store, then to the mall where we arranged to have our home phone and internet connected. We bought a dish rack and a bath mat, then stopped along the way at a liquor store. Back at home we made a large meal, set up a table on the back porch, and ate dinner as the sun went down. We stayed up late drinking wine in the dark. When I finally went to bed, I had a hard time winding down. I tossed and turned for a while, thinking how everything was different now. From just yesterday, into this. From the life I'd been living these past few months, into this. And what is this? I wondered, drifting off to sleep.

In the following days I met Elliot for the first time. It happened when Annie took me to visit his place. He and his roommate Chris had rented a two-bedroom suite on the ground floor of a townhouse. Upstairs was a young family with a newborn baby whose nursery was right over Elliot's room. We spent a while listening to the baby cry, and to the mother as she tried singing it to sleep. On his desk, Elliot had a pile of paper clips, so while we were sitting there I twisted and bent them into animal shapes. I made two elephants, a few giraffes and then a handful of trees which I arranged into a kind of forest scene. Of course, I was only doing it to avoid having to talk—to avoid having to look Elliot in the eyes—while the baby cried above us.

Later that night Elliot and Chris came to our house. Chris was sullen, quiet. He gave the impression of having been dragged along. He hardly spoke a word, even as we drank wine and smoked a joint to try and break the ice. Meanwhile, Annie and Elliot talked to each other like a pair of old friends. They spoke eagerly about people in the city, people they somehow knew in common, as if they had so much catching up to do. As usual, I drank too much and the wine went straight to my head. At one point in the evening, Elliot and I wound up in the kitchen, just the two of us, standing in a nook by the sink, close because of the fact that the cupboards didn't allow much room. And who knows what we said to each other. Maybe we talked about cigarettes, and about how I had started smoking them recently. Elliot thought it was a dumb thing to do, for someone my age to start such an awful, nasty habit, but I tried to convince him that maybe it wasn't dumb, not if you really thought about it, and not if you considered the reasons I had for having started. I went on to tell him what those reasons were, certain that he was coming on to me, showing me a kind of interest that went beyond what I was saying as I talked and talked.

Soon it was September and we were into the beginning of classes. The days already seemed shorter and the nights were growing cold. By then the initial excitement of being back again had started to fade, and once it had faded, once I was able to see things more for what they were, I realized that something had changed between Annie and me.

At first I noticed little things that I hadn't ever noticed before. How Annie projected something of a special significance onto our friendship, how she acted as though we alone were in on a conspiracy together, as though we alone were able to recognize and communicate the cosmic absurdity of life. Maybe in the past I'd enjoyed this game, but now it struck me as an affectation. That a woman in the grocery store would be buying apples all the way from Peru, that a professor in his middle age would admit he had never read a poem he liked, or that wild poppies would grow and bloom out of cracks at the side of the road—these foibles and miracles were what Annie would use to try and bind us together asking: Do you see this? Now I couldn't help but feel these were nothing more than regular occurrences, simply ordinary, completely mundane. And her insistence that they carry a significance had become annoying and bothersome.

It was like Annie and I were stuck on different pages. It was like we had skipped a beat and the rhythm had been broken between us. The trouble was that we never happened to speak about it, although she must have recognized it too. It remained as a kind of embarrassment, looming on the edges of our friendship.

Then something happened one Saturday night around the middle of the month. Annie, Chris, Elliot and I went to a party. Chris was his usual sullen self, but Annie took it upon herself to try and coax him out of his shell. She spent the whole night dragging him around and introducing him to the people she knew. Meanwhile, Elliot and I snuck away on our own.

The party was in a large house that had about ten different people renting rooms in it. We spent a while snooping, going into people's bedrooms and opening drawers. I was glad to see Elliot could get into this, exploring people's personal spaces without them knowing it, studying the objects they kept, but without any inclination to steal or disrupt anything. Eventually we wandered outside into the yard. In a dark corner there was a tree with excellent low-hanging branches for climbing. We hoisted ourselves up and perched there side by side. We leaned together, pressed our bodies and faces together until finally we kissed. Then Elliot told me that he and Annie had fallen in love. He told me what a beautiful person Annie was, how genuinely good, how tender and human and warm. Then we kissed again, so hard this time that I split my lip.

And what about Franklin? What had happened to him?

By now I understood that he and Annie weren't together. As for what had happened, or when it had happened, nobody told me anything. It occurred to me that Annie and I never spoke about things that weren't light and easy. On one hand it didn't surprise me that she'd never spoken about her breakup with Franklin. On the other, it seemed odd that in all the time she'd been without him, and in all her emails and the words we'd exchanged, she never mentioned anything.

Franklin was around, though. He was living in the city, with his parents, and going to school. At least once he had been to the house, only a few nights after we had moved in. Apparently he and Annie were still friends, and still saw each other now and again.

By chance, Franklin and I were enrolled in one of the same courses, The Existential Philosophers: Their Lives, Their Works.

The professor was an older woman, small and thin, with a biting intellect. Franklin and I both admired her and grew to appreciate the course. There were two time slots for it though, one early in the morning, the other immediately afterward. Franklin always went to the early class, and even though I wanted to see him, I was never able to pull myself out of bed.

One afternoon around the end of the month, Franklin turned up at the door to our house. I was alone, not expecting anyone, and so I was confused when I opened the door and saw him. I told him Annie wasn't home, that she had gone out somewhere with Elliot, but Franklin said he was here to see me.

Still confused, I invited him in. We wound up in the living room where there was a couch, a small side table and a lamp, but otherwise no other furniture, no adornment of any kind. Franklin said, I love what you've done with the place.

I figured he was joking but explained the philosophy we had followed in dealing with the size of the house. Annie and I didn't own enough to fill the space, but rather than to leave rooms entirely empty, we'd decided to spread ourselves and our possessions, however thinly, throughout. This way we could say we were living here, that we were in touch with every part of the house. In lieu of any response to my explanation, Franklin took an exaggerated stride across the living room.

I suddenly felt awkward. I asked Franklin if he wanted to step outside, if he wanted to climb onto the roof. Walking through the kitchen and out the back, I explained that I'd been sitting on the roof sometimes to smoke. There was a ladder in the yard which I had propped against the wall.

Did I tell you I've been smoking cigarettes? It's only because I like to smoke, I said, but I don't always want to be high.

Franklin nodded, then we climbed up the ladder to a more or less flat spot on the roof where we could sit with our legs hanging over the eaves.

There's a reason I'm here, Franklin told me.

I lit a cigarette. I didn't offer him one.

I want to ask you something, he said. I want to ask if you'll be my confidant.

I confessed I didn't know what that was.

A confidant is someone you can tell your secrets to. It's someone you can trust, someone who will listen to what you have to say.

So, I said, it's like a friend.

It's like a friend, said Franklin, but one of a particular kind.

Okay then, I'll do it, I said. I will be your confidant.

Franklin took a deep breath and started to talk, first about his travels in Europe, saying it had felt good being with Annie then. It had felt right, he said, and he'd known he was in love with her. But then she'd needed to come home and Franklin had wanted to travel on, so he had seen her off at an airport in Lyon and then travelled back to Greece to spend time on the islands there. Now that he was alone, Franklin said it had felt right and good to be alone. It had felt right at first in Greece, and then on into other countries. Then after Europe, coming home, it had still felt right and good.

Franklin spent the summer working idly at a part-time job in the city, and for a whole two months, he and Annie were barely in touch. Franklin had hardly written to her, and never once tried to get her on the phone. He had more or less forgotten her and, he said, forgotten he had ever been in love with her. In the meantime, Annie was broken-hearted, but then she met Elliot and they became friends. Then late one night at his parents' house, while God only knows what record played, she and Elliot kissed and fooled around, and she forgot all about her love-sickness.

As soon as I saw her again, I remembered that I was in love, said Franklin. It only took a few minutes, really. I only had to see her move, to see her speak, and then it felt real all over again. I realized that it had been foolish, silly of me to forget. I asked her if we could start over again.

But she said no, I said. Obviously.

Why obviously?

Well, it seems she's in love with somebody else.

With Elliot. Yes, it seems that way.

I asked Franklin, Have you ever met Elliot?

Once, he said, but it was brief. He's a very handsome man.

After that, we fell into a short silence and the world around us was silent too. I remember thinking that this was the silence that falls between people who understand each other perfectly, when between them there's nothing more that needs to be said. I pointed into the neighbouring yard.

Over there is a kid who's maybe eight or nine years old, I said. Just a little boy, and he must just be learning the trumpet. His parents make him practise in the yard, so I've seen him out here a handful of times, standing in a very formal way, with a posture that someone must have taught him in school. He looks very proper, steady and focused. He lifts his horn, holds it up, presses his lips into it, and then he blows a single note. He brings his trumpet down again, takes a breath, then raises it up, and it's the same thing all over again, but a different note. Over and over again. It's really weird and an amazing thing to see. It's something I can't quite figure out. I mean, he's doing this for hours at a time, playing just a note at a time, one after another. It's as if he's trying to make a perfect sound, but there isn't any music, you know? There isn't any music to keep him going.

I lit another cigarette. Still Franklin didn't speak. There was another silence, and I remember this time thinking that maybe we didn't understand each other, that maybe we were only two people, terribly separate and far apart.

Will you be my confidant? I asked.

Franklin hesitated, and immediately I regretted having asked. It was as if, for having done him the favour of listening, I now expected that favour returned.

I kissed Elliot, I said. Or maybe he kissed me, who knows?

If Franklin was at all surprised, it didn't show. Calm and sensible, he asked, When did this happen?

It was two weeks ago.

Does Annie know about it?

She doesn't, I said.

Franklin asked, Is it going to happen again?

We decided it wouldn't, it shouldn't, it won't.

After a while, as if he was thinking out loud, Franklin said, I wonder if we could ever be friends.

I thought we were confidants, I said.

We are, but I meant with Elliot. I wonder if he and I could ever be friends.

Franklin and I stayed on the roof for as long as it took for the sun to sink and for shadows to grow and smother the yard. Mosquito bites bloomed on our arms and legs.

Do you want to get high? I asked, throwing away the cigarette I had just lit. These don't always do it for me.

Franklin said he wasn't smoking pot these days. He explained that he was trying to keep a level head. When it was time for him to go, we climbed down the ladder and I walked him again through the house. At the door, he shook my hand. I laughed.

I probably haven't shaken hands with a man since the last time I did with you, I said.

But Franklin didn't laugh. He just stood there, and after shaking my hand he thanked me. For what exactly, I wasn't sure.

Sometimes I wondered what Annie saw in me. She had so many other friends and could have been living with anyone, but she turned to me, she chose me, and I just didn't understand. As a person, I wasn't the type to appeal to Annie's sensibilities. In other friends and in the stories she told, in the worlds she'd conveyed in her letters, I could never find any trace of myself. It caused me to wonder if she even knew who I was, or if she'd maybe been mistaken at some point along the way. Really, we had only known each other for a few seasons now, and although we'd been close, we'd never seen each other change or grow. At least, not until now, I thought.

It was obvious our relationship was coming apart, and although I blamed myself, I didn't feel regret. In truth, I didn't care. I blamed myself only as a matter of course, because something or somebody had to be blamed, and I didn't mind really, bearing that cross. I felt such a bitterness toward her and was constantly annoyed with the fact that she didn't notice, or that she refused to see what was happening. Out of the blue she'd turn to me and say: Elliot's very intrigued with you. She would say: Elliot likes you. He talks about you all the time.

As for Franklin, I didn't see him as often as I'd like. When I did, it was only in passing. Him coming out of the early session of our course on the existentialists, me going into the later one. I wanted for us to sit together and talk. I tried to stop him in the hallway to say hello. I would try to make a joke, but our conversations were always clipped and full of hesitation. Franklin was distracted. He looked sad. He looked uneasy, like he didn't want to see me. I didn't take it personally. I figured I reminded him of things he would rather forget.

The days were short and the nights were long. I was staying up late, and the rains came. On Halloween I dressed as a doll with my hair tied into a bun, my cheeks and lips painted red. Elliot was Humpty Dumpty. He'd given himself a paunch and wore suspenders with a helmet painted white like an egg. I remember Chris's costume too, although I thought it was a lazy one. He went dressed in his regular clothes, but with a carved-out pumpkin on his head. We went to a party that night, and at some point someone pulled the pumpkin off his head, and smashed it to pieces on the living room floor. I remember Chris standing over the remains of the pumpkin looking defeated, overwhelmed at the senselessness of what had happened. But the party was like that—things got broken, drinks were spilled. The neighbours complained about the noise, and eventually felt they had to call the police. I mean, it was a sloppy night, one that brought out the worst in us all.

Now, I scratch my head, wrack my brain, but try as I might, I can't remember anymore how Annie was dressed. At any rate, I remember that she was morose. This wasn't a party well suited to her. It wasn't suited to anyone, but especially not to Annie since it jarred against her notion of the basic decency of others. That night she wound up drunk. She fought with Elliot. He tried to kiss me several times while she was out of the room, but I dodged him. I took the high road, insisting that he did too. Eventually Annie said something about walking to the ends of the Earth and disappeared. Only later I learned that she wound up puking by the side of the road and falling asleep on a neighbour's lawn.

Soon the police arrived and started emptying bottles, dispersing the crowd. Annie was gone. Chris was nowhere to be found. And then, just as I was wondering what I should do, Elliot grabbed me by the hand and led me down the driveway into the street. He didn't let go of my hand, but kept pulling me down the street, away from the party, away from the noise.

What are we doing? I asked him.

I don't know for sure, he said.

I told him I needed a pack of cigarettes, and so it was decided he would walk me to a store, but it quickly became apparent we weren't headed for a store, nor to any place in particular. We wound up wandering and talking about Annie. He talked about their relationship, how it hadn't been good in a while. That it wasn't working anymore was obvious, but he said that Annie refused to admit it. Later we had found a little beach and were sitting on a log together, tight together, close as a way to stay warm.

Do me a favour. Do to me now like I did to you before, I said.

What'd you do to me before?

I resisted you, I said.

I kissed him, but he didn't resist. Instead, we pressed into each other, trying to get as close as was humanly possible. We pressed into each other urgent and hard, like separated lovers coming together at last.

That was the end of something, like the unravelling of a story that had gone on too long and had become awkward to tell. There were no surprises here. There was nothing to hide and no lessons for any of us to carry away. It was like a ringing of bells and nothing more.

After it had come to light what Elliot and I had done, Annie left the house and took a leave of absence from her classes. She left the city and stayed for a while with her parents, at least until she was well enough to return. She even had herself excused from writing several of her midterm exams, and I had to wonder what excuse she'd given, or whether the university had simply accepted the truth, that she was suffering yet another broken heart.

One Friday night, as I was sitting in the living room, Franklin came by the house with no other reason but to see me. I told him about an email that Annie had sent in which she'd mentioned she was having thoughts of killing herself.

And what did you respond to that? Franklin asked.

I told her I was scared, I said, scared to hear her thinking that way.

So you lied?

Of course, I said. Anyway, she's being ridiculous. She doesn't really want to end her life, she's only saying so because to her it's a novel idea. What she doesn't understand is that everybody thinks about it, practically all the time.

You think about it?

Of course I do. Everybody does. But I'm not going to do it, and neither will she.

If you don't think she'll do it, then why lie? asked Franklin.

Well, I said, what's the point of rubbing salt in her wound?

Franklin seemed to think about this. But, he said, in some way isn't your dishonesty the wound she's had to suffer?

Sure, but Annie doesn't really want honesty. She can't even be honest with herself.

It does seem unlikely she would ever kill herself, Franklin said. But it is probably for the best you didn't tell her that.

It was an honourable lie, I said.

Sure, if such a thing as honour exists.

We went on like this for a while, talking in the living room, sitting at opposite ends of the couch. I had my legs curled up beneath me to keep my feet warm. Franklin, on the other hand, was wearing his coat. He had both feet planted on the floor as if he were sitting in a waiting room. After a while, he suggested we get stoned.

I thought you were off it these days, I said.

Was I? Franklin asked and shrugged.

The trouble, I explained, was that I had had a cough all week, and what had started merely as a tickle in the throat had moved and settled into my chest. So, I didn't want to smoke. But I did have some butter in the fridge which had been infused with cannabis. It was a gift to Annie from one of her friends, which she had intended to use to make brownies. In her absence though, I told Franklin, I've been spreading it on crackers and eating it as a regular snack. I could make us some crackers, I told him.

How about a smoothie? Franklin countered.

Twenty minutes later we had ingested the drugs along with some berries, banana, honey and almond milk. Now we wondered what to do with the night. Franklin wanted to meet up with friends, but I didn't want to see anyone. I still didn't know any of Franklin's friends, and didn't want to be introduced to them. It made me wonder about the nature of our relationship, but to my mind, Franklin existed as someone outside of all social context. He was someone who had fallen into my life, someone who had found his way, unattached, into an otherwise empty house.

Franklin dialled several numbers but couldn't get a hold of anyone. I was relieved. The truth was I would have been content for us to spend the whole night in the living room. Franklin suggested we go for a drive. He had his father's blue sports car parked outside in the driveway, and since I couldn't readily think up an excuse not to go, that's what we did.

Franklin started driving and I felt nervous because I didn't know where we were going. He drove into the city, over a bridge, into the industrial zone, then downtown and beyond, following the coast. He took us onto the highway and then off it again, and while we weren't talking and while I wasn't thinking about anything in particular, I realized that the anxiety I felt had to do with Annie and Elliot. It was in the background of every moment now, this feeling that life could be dangerous, that people could be hurt, could be damaged. That I could be responsible. Who knows, I thought, if Franklin and I might not do something reckless.

After driving aimlessly for an hour, we left the city, and it was only then that I felt relief. A physical warmth came over me, a comfort growing from the pit of my stomach. We headed north up the coast, through an old-growth forest, winding at the foot of a mountain.

We drove for many hours and only started talking again as the landscape changed. Franklin, seemingly unprovoked, told me about a woman Nietzsche had loved named Lou Andreas-Salomé. Nietzsche had even proposed to her, but she hadn't wanted to get married. In fact, she'd been opposed to it on philosophical grounds. So, the two of them had a falling out. Later Salomé married someone else and then had an affair with the poet Rainer Maria Rilke.

Even though she'd been married, Franklin explained, by the time of the affair, she'd already been celibate for a number of years, in accordance with her philosophical principles. Rilke though, at least for a while, changed all that. He was fourteen years younger than her and their affair lasted almost three years. Salomé was the one to break it off, but the two of them remained close. They shared an intimate friendship lasting well over a decade.

What intrigues me, Franklin said, is just how fitting it is to each of those men.

What do you mean? I asked.

Just how in keeping it is with who they were. Can't you picture, for instance, Friedrich retreating with a broken heart, defeated and embittered, fleeing into seclusion to philosophize with a hammer? And Rilke, on the other hand, staying close to the woman, close to the situation, potentially painful, but also beautiful and apparently potent?

Apparently?

Judging by the friendship they forged from it, said Franklin.

Okay, I said, I get it. But my question is, who was she?

Salomé? She was a writer, a poet, a philosopher.

I didn't say anything then. I thought that something must be missing from the story, but I couldn't guess what it was.

Franklin asked if Annie knew that I was still seeing Elliot. He said, Elliot is a very handsome man. You two would make gorgeous babies.

It's true, he's a good-looking man, I said. I rested my head against the window.

We drove until we reached the next town, several hours up the road. Franklin pulled up at the local rink where there was a hockey game being played between teams made up of teenage boys. We went in, bought coffee in Styrofoam cups and sat with the other spectators. These were mostly parents of the players, also groups of friends and girlfriends. Franklin chose to side with the team in blue and cheered them exuberantly. He called out: Let's go boys! Let's take these bozos to the cleaners! No one else in the place was shouting and pretty soon the players themselves were looking up in our direction.

During a break in the play, Franklin told me he had kissed Julia.

You remember Julia? he said. She's an old friend. You went to her house for a party last spring.

Right, I said. Of course, Julia. The girl with the enormous eyes.

I never noticed before. I guess you could say her eyes are big, Franklin said.

Not big. Enormous. Her eyes are these grand, spectacular things.

I've known her since the first grade, Franklin said. She's been one of my oldest, closest friends. Then, I don't know why, but I wound up kissing her yesterday.

And what was that like? I asked.

It was a little bit strange.

A week or two later, Annie came home, and things were almost as they'd been before. For a few days, we were back to being friends, spending evenings talking about nothing, being stoned together and getting carried away.

One night we had an idea to trace every shadow in one of the rooms in the basement. The room was full of junk left over from previous tenants. It was the only room in the house that was full, packed to the rafters with boxes, books, rusted pots and pans, old bicycle tires. Whenever we turned on the light, all this junk would cast an array of shadows over the walls and the floor. We went in there with a box of sidewalk chalk and spent a few hours tracing the shadows. It felt good to be working together, with nothing more between us than our concern that we might not have enough chalk to finish. When we were done, we emptied the room to see the effect of our work. Annie took a few pictures, but then she said she was tired. She went to bed and I waited, then after I figured she'd fallen asleep, I slipped out the back of the house and started the long walk over to Elliot's place.

When I arrived, I told him all about the shadows, the chalk, about working with Annie. Looking betrayed, he asked me how I could do that. To be Annie's friend, and then the next moment be pulling back the sheets on his bed?

I don't understand, he said, whether you're cheating on me, or cheating on her.

I don't think I'm cheating on anyone.

But you are lying, he said.

He was right, but by now all of this had come to seem so inevitable to me, so unexceptional, that more than anything else, I felt tired of it. Could I have been gentler, perhaps more considerate? Sure. Could I have chosen to behave in a different way? Of course. But what was the point? These things had already fallen into place, had taken shape, and who was I to resist?

All I'm doing is putting one foot in front of the other, I said.

In Elliot's room there was a tape deck with a few cassettes that he and I had played over and over. One was Billie Holiday singing "All of Me" and other songs. I knew then that these songs would be drilled into me, that years later I would hear them and be taken back into Elliot's room. Whenever a cassette needed to be flipped, we took turns. One of us would get out of bed and cross the room to the stereo. And at that time it was no small thing to be naked, standing, while the other one watched. When it was my turn, I padded quickly and nervously over the floor. I stood at the stereo with my back to him, and when I turned, he was sitting up watching me. I stood there practically frozen.

You look good, Elliot said. You're a very beautiful girl. Even more so, the more I get to see of you.

The first time we slept together we brought all the blankets down onto the floor. When it was over we brought them back to the bed. Elliot started the cassette and I fell asleep, only to wake up hours later as the sky was already blue. For a moment I felt such a deep sense of satisfaction, and I knew that whatever would happen in life, I would do anything, would give anything to feel this way again.

Things quickly degraded between Annie and me. Sometimes she would come to my room, knock at the door, and when I didn't answer, come in anyway and find me lying on the floor. Evidently she wanted to talk. Or, she wanted me to talk. But what did she expect? Some kind of an explanation? Some display of remorse?

The truth is I didn't feel any remorse. I knew I probably should, but whenever I went looking, it just wasn't there. So Annie would lie down next to me, both of us on the floor, neither of us saying anything.

Once, after I thought she'd gone to bed, I got ready to leave the house again, but this time Annie met me on my way out the door. Standing in the entrance together, I could see that she had an umbrella in her hands.

You should take this, she said. It's going to rain.

I shook my head. I don't need it.

But it's going to rain, she said.

If it rains, I'll get wet. I'll be fine.

I walked the length of our road for half an hour before the sky opened up, at which point I turned and went back home. When I got in, she was sitting in the living room.

I didn't expect you back, she admitted. I thought, you know...

I know what you thought, but I was just taking a walk.

Annie sighed, but it was more like a groan. Sometimes I'm still so mad at you, she said.

I nodded.

You sold my piano.

I looked up at her, ready to laugh, but I could see it wasn't a joke.

A few days later she left again.

It was December now, and time to prepare for exams. Franklin and I got together once or twice with the goal of studying the existentialists. We met on campus, found a quiet spot, opened our notes and books, but inevitably fell into talk of other things. Our relationship had cemented itself, had evolved into something independent of Annie. We were getting along. We enjoyed each other's company.

On the night before the exam, Franklin invited himself to the house. He suggested we spend the evening studying, then get a good night's sleep, and in the morning drive to the university. Since Annie was away, Franklin would spend the night sleeping in her room.

He came by just after dark, toting an overnight bag. The first thing he wanted to do was to put his bag away in the room. We opened up Annie's bedroom door, turned on the light and went inside. Franklin took a few steps, then fell face down on the bed. He took a deep breath and sighed.

As usual, Annie had somehow managed to make her bedroom nicer than the rest of the house. The room was comfortable and inviting, and although she hadn't been living here in weeks, the place was still fragrant and warm.

Franklin sat up on the bed. He said, I know I told you I wasn't, but I think I'm in love with Annie again.

Really? I asked. Since when?

Since maybe just now, he said.

I turned away and started poking around the room, looking for a distraction. On the window sill was a photo of Annie's parents and her younger brother. Next to it was a long grey feather and a bluish, small, round stone. On the wall next to the window was a calendar still set to the previous month.

I lifted the page, and speaking over my shoulder said to Franklin, She'll be coming back in three more days.

Will the two of you be able to sort things out?

I didn't answer. When I turned around I saw that Franklin had a book in his hands, Rilke's *Letters to a Young Poet*. He started reading out loud.

It is good to love, because love is difficult. That is why young people, who are beginners in everything, are not yet capable of love: it is something they must learn. But learning time is always a long, secluded time ahead—is solitude, intensified. Loving does not mean at first merging, surrendering and uniting with another person—for what would a union be of two people who are unclarified, unfinished and still incoherent?

I read that to Annie once, Franklin said after a pause. It was when we were in Greece and she was so wild about Rilke. We used to read it to each other every night before bed, and in the morning we would talk about what we had read. I asked her about that particular passage but she said she didn't remember it. She said she must have fallen asleep.

Franklin continued to read from the book, but quietly, only to himself.

I wish she wouldn't come back, I said. Again, I had turned away from the bed. I didn't know if Franklin was listening. I've spent the last three nights with Elliot, and I'll be with him again tomorrow, and I just can't tell you how good it is just to fall asleep in his bed. I woke up this morning and I didn't need to worry about Annie or about anything else. I didn't need to hurry or sneak around. It's like, how can I describe it? It's like I've almost got something, something so basic and ordinary, and like it's almost real. I can hold it, almost, just as long as she doesn't come home. For as long as she's away I can pretend that it's mine and that it really exists.

I turned and saw that Franklin had swung his legs off the bed.

We should study, he said. Then he started taking books out of his bag.

We spread our notes on the kitchen table and tried for a while to study. Franklin started coughing, though, complaining that there was too much dust in this old house. Before I could say anything, he went into the bathroom to blow his nose. I even heard him splash water on his face.

After that we tried to go on studying, but Franklin kept coughing and getting up. He rubbed his eyes until they were red, and it became clear we wouldn't get anything done.

Maybe it's for the best, said Franklin. I don't think I should stay here tonight after all.

Really? I said. You're going to go home?

It's because of the dust, he said.

The next thing I knew Franklin had packed his things, had grabbed his bag out of Annie's room and was on his way to the door. He paused on the landing only long enough to say good-bye. And just like that, he was gone.

I never believed it was Franklin's allergies that drove him away that night, but I can't say I know for sure what it was. Maybe he was overwhelmed and didn't want to sleep in Annie's bed. Maybe I had finally offended him. Maybe I had hurt him with my callousness, set against the woman he loved. Anyway, that night he behaved in a way I had never seen him behave before. He shut himself off, he ran away and left me standing there, without an explanation. Maybe it was just the dust.

After Franklin left I tried going back to my study notes but the effort didn't last very long. Eventually I packed up my things, turned out the kitchen light and went around turning out every other light in the house. Finally, I wound up sitting in the living room. There was enough glare coming in at the windows that I could sit in the dark and still see fairly well. Not that there was anything to see.

I had some pot in my dresser, but I figured if I wasn't going to study, I shouldn't get stoned. I lit a cigarette instead and let the ashes fall into a pile on the floor. There was a bottle of wine in the kitchen, so I thought I might have a glass of that. I put on some music and had another glass. I went for a walk and brought the whole bottle along. In the end, I spent half that night sitting on the living room floor, drinking wine and drawing shapes with the tip of my finger in a mixture of ashes and dust.

WAR STORY

The baby woke us up around one, and my wife got out of bed with him because it was her turn. I think she nursed him, but I quickly fell asleep. The next thing I knew she was shaking my foot with a free hand, and I couldn't quite make sense of what was happening. I looked at the clock and saw that more than an hour had passed, which meant she'd been up with him all this time, going room to room through the apartment, rocking him and singing to him, trying to keep him from crying, trying to get him to sleep. I got up and pulled on a shirt, found my jeans in a pile on the floor and put them on. At some point in the last two weeks I had learned that the only way to get the baby to sleep at a time like this, in the middle of the night, when every other recourse had failed, was to take him for a walk around the neighbourhood.

I stood at the top of the stairs, and with Henry in my arms, and without bending down, tried to shimmy a foot into my canvas shoe. My kitchen shoes were also by the door, and they were more comfortable and easier too to slip on, but being as they were coated underfoot with a layer of grease, they presented something of a hazard, something to be avoided while descending our stairs in the dark with a one-month old babe in my arms. As I stood there refusing to take a chance in those shoes, I gave myself a mental congratulations. After all, this was proof I was maturing. I was learning. I was being responsible.

We were still new to Montreal, having moved here in the winter while my wife had been pregnant. She hadn't known that she was pregnant at the time. If she'd have known, we never would have moved, she never would have come. She hated Montreal and I respected her for that because she, I thought, was a rare kind of animal.

Everyone I'd ever met had been enamoured with the place, as I was too. The red brick, the iron stairs, particularly those in our neighbourhood, with balconies overhanging the street, and even trees locked into their little plots on the sidewalk—every little piece of it had me enthralled.

Out at two or three in the morning, it was calm and quiet. Being summer, it was warm. So warm that my son could be dressed in pajamas and I could walk with him simply cradled in my arms as if the city was ours, belonged to us, as if the world was our living room.

Up Saint-Philippe to Notre-Dame, past the tattoo parlours and the mattress stores, the marchés aux puces with their doors caged for the night. As usual, we walked past the Café Riviera and stopped and stood for a while. Through the big front windows we studied the pattern of shadows and light on the floor. I tried to explain to Henry that this was where I worked, that here was the place I spent my days. This is where your Dad goes when he isn't at home, I said to his incomprehension. This is where I am when I'm gone away (and here I shifted him to release one arm, and with my free hand made a gesture like a bird flying away).

We crossed the street and went into the park, which was where he would always fall asleep, his eyes growing heavy, looking up into the trees. Tonight was as usual. Henry drifted off as we rounded the fountain. I knew that now I could go home if I wanted. I could put him down and put myself to bed, but I decided instead to keep going, to walk at least until I reached the canal. After all, I was already up, and despite the hour, it felt good to be out. It felt like nothing really mattered, as if in all of life there was nothing more important than this, nothing of greater significance. Just to be walking in the night with my son in my arms.

The next morning I'd need to be up by six, and I'd be tired but okay with it. It was summer now anyway, so every morning was bright and it felt almost good to be up and about. Walking to work, I would take the back streets. Down Sainte-Marguerite and once again through the park. I would believe I could feel the whole city also coming to life, waking out of its slumber. I'd be almost inspired to be a part of this massive, daily movement of people, getting out of bed and into the world. Meanwhile, I was a cook in a small café, so I had my own role to play. While they were getting ready to walk out the door, I'd be brushing their morning pastry. Then, while they were at their offices, eyes deep in screens, I'd be putting together their lunch. Fine feelings, I had then, but of course those wouldn't last. Because doesn't every summer have to come to an end? This one was no different. It began with a chill. The mornings were fresh, then brisk, then cold. Leaves began to turn in the park and pretty soon it was dark as I was getting out of bed. And though it was still bright walking down along Sainte-Marguerite on my way to the café, it was bright with a sun that didn't offer any warmth.

One morning while approaching the café, I spied one of our baristas on the patio. She was sitting with her back against the wall, her legs stretched out in front of her and smoking a cigarette with her eyes closed while a dappled light played against her face. Her name was Emily and she had a reputation for being kind of brainy. I think it was only because she had recently graduated with an honours degree in literature, and given the state of the economy or whatnot, she had wound up so far only working here. As I approached her, I shook the keys to the café from my pocket. When Emily opened her eyes, I spoke.

It looked as if you were lost in thought, I said. Sorry to interrupt.

Emily said something that was evidently a quote. That time of year thou mayest in me behold, she said, when yellow leaves, or none, or few do hang…

That word "yellow" made me think of the particular light of these mornings, and I figured that what Emily had said was meant to refer in some way to this season, and to the particular way in which it went creeping into the mind, taking its effect.

It's Shakespeare, Emily said.

No. I mean, of course it is, I said.

There was an awkward moment, and whatever I'd been thinking, I couldn't recover it now. Being unable to explain that a misunderstanding had just occurred, I capitulated.

That was lovely, I said.

I asked Emily what she was doing here since it had just occurred to me that as this morning's barista, she didn't need to be in for another half hour. Emily waved her hand in the air and the smoke of her cigarette did a little dance.

I was awake, she said, so I thought I might as well come in.

I nodded, and stepping past her, opened the side door into the kitchen. At that time it didn't seem at all strange that someone would want to come in early for their shift. The café still had a kind of warmth and a quality of easy-goingness. Of course, all of that too would change, and only a few weeks later, Emily's eagerness, or say her willingness to get to work, would seem almost unthinkable.

When I'd started working at the café, the situation had been that the owners were in charge of our daily operations. Vincent and Valerie were in their mid-thirties and were remarkably well established, both for their age and for the type of people they were. It was Vincent's family, I supposed, that owned the building which housed the café. Above us was his brother's apartment, and still above that was another apartment, this one belonging to Vincent, Valerie and to their toddler-aged son, Napoli.

It had been Valerie's project to open the café. She'd been a chef for more than a dozen years working in various restaurants and some hotels. When I first arrived, she was running the kitchen, but then in the following months, eased herself out of the position, wanting instead to focus on becoming a yoga instructor. Truth is, I was glad when she left. Valerie could be sweet at times, even kind, warm and generous, but there were days during which she slipped into inscrutable moods, when she would enter the café in a hoodie with sunglasses over her eyes, when she would make herself a coffee and a light snack, then stand in the kitchen and manage to slip a few barbs into whoever was working, saying that what they were doing was wrong, all wrong, and that they would need to do it over again. What a shame, what a waste, what a stupid mistake, she would say, and then leave as quickly as she'd come.

When Val started training in yoga, she made a rule for herself not to enter the kitchen. She didn't even want to know what was happening there. Her removal from the job had to be total, she'd said. So from that point on, Vincent took over, although he had no background in this kind of work. Essentially, he left those of us working in the café to our own devices, only coming into the kitchen occasionally, always late in the morning, and looking as if he had just woken up. Invariably, Napoli would be riding on his hip, the boy dressed in a T-shirt with no bottoms, no diaper, his bare bum pressed into the meat of Vincent's arm. On such occasions, Vincent's great contribution to our work was usually to describe a late-night sandwich he had eaten recently at a place on Rue Saint-Laurent. At one of those charcuterie places, he would explain. It had roast chicken, tomato sauce and I think maybe some swiss? And it was simple, but like real fucking food, you know? Like the kind of thing that makes you want to start a family, that makes you want to build a house.

Then Vincent would wonder if we could add something like that to our menu. Of course, everyone knew to ignore such requests since it had happened time and again that when one of us did put in the effort, say to visit Saint-Laurent to eat a sandwich and then attempt to create a facsimile, by the time we'd been able to put it together, Vincent would have already moved on, forgotten entirely that the suggestion for this sandwich had been his, and would dismiss our work with something like: It isn't Italian enough.

As a result, those of us working in the café learned to manage ourselves. We were in charge of the menu, and of ordering stock.

We were responsible for seeing that nothing got wasted, and that there were sufficient quantities to meet the shifting demands of the day. It was up to us cooks to keep the kitchen running smoothly, and the same was true of the baristas in the front of the house. If there were any conflicts, it was our job to solve them, or at least to behave in a reasonable way. To work things out amongst ourselves.

All of this was hard, and of course some of us did better than others, but everything that happened each day resulted directly from the work we put in. Every success belonged to us. And in this arrangement, we each felt a great deal of freedom, too. We were allowed to organize our time and invent our own methods for getting things done. We were free to create and to improvise. We were free to be lost in our work. For me, it was a feeling I hadn't ever had at a job in the past, and I didn't know it was possible.

But all of that changed in October, when Vincent and Valerie hired a manager. Not only did they hire a manager, they hired the worst possible person to come and take charge of the situation. Teresa was in her forties, and like Valerie, she had worked for a decade at a slew of different places around the city. Before that, she'd been living in Toronto. She admitted she still felt out of place here. She didn't know her way around the city at all, and she didn't speak a word of French. That on its own should have been a strike against her, seeing that more than half the members of our staff were francophones.

Practically overnight, Teresa turned the prevailing scene at the café from something light to something heavy, from easy to anxious, something now tinged with paranoia. One of her first decrees was that from now on, everyone in the kitchen would need to wear a uniform. From now on, we would need to wear a white coat, black pants and a tidy black cap on our heads. But it wasn't just the uniform that irked, after all the coat and pants and even those caps had always been available to us on a rack in the basement if we'd wanted them, but it was the principle of now being told what to wear, the inflexibility of Teresa's demand, and the pettiness with which it was enforced that made the difference. We were given to understand that from now on, Vincent and Valerie wanted nothing more to do with the business of running the café, and so they vested their authority in Teresa. And forget it if you wanted to complain. They would turn a blind ear, a cold shoulder, and would tell you that whatever your problem was, take it up with the boss.

Teresa's position was by default defensive. Her expression was invariably stiff, her eyes calculating and scrutinizing. In every conversation, she came forward bearing arms. It was as if she were always prepared to do battle, and she wanted you to see it. She wanted you to recognize this about her because it was a challenge and a threat and a warning on her part.

For a group like us who had grown accustomed to our liberties, it was unnerving to have someone peering over your shoulder while you worked, to have someone correcting your work, and mostly for reasons that seemed arbitrary, to have a person with little else to do than exercise authority and a lot of people couldn't take it. Some of us were fired for trying to stand up to her. Others simply quit, either because they couldn't stand to work with her, or because they were able to read the writing on the wall and see that what the café had been, it would no longer be. It was as if the job you thought you had was suddenly taken away and replaced with something else altogether. For those of us who did remain, it was hard to see so many coworkers fall, bizarre to witness an influx of new employees, and disappointing—but also gratifying—to then see those new hires quickly turn against Teresa too. It was dizzying to see all of this happen so fast, but then what could you do other than to come into work every day?

Ricky was another cook, and something of a friend. He'd been working at the café for only a couple of months when Teresa fired him. He and I had been working the weekend shift. Teresa never worked the weekend shift, so Ricky and I enjoyed an oasis without her. Every weekend, the café was as it had been before Teresa. People were relaxed, cheerful and talkative. Ricky went around cracking jokes and singing songs. He was a musician, actually. He wasn't a cook at all, although he worked as one. Music was really what he cared about.

Between Ricky and I, more than anything else, there was a difference of circumstance. Because here we were: me with my early nights and platitudes, doing things in life like trying not to drink as much alcohol anymore, while Ricky was this guy who had two smoking pistols tattooed on his forearm, their barrels crossed and the name Marita written in smoke as an homage to his grandfather. At home, he had trays of psilocybin mushrooms growing in a bedroom closet. Every week he showed me pictures of the progress they had made, scrolling dotingly through entire albums on his phone. So we were in different places, but we were comfortable. We fell into a kind of rhythm, working together.

At the end of each day, I would let Ricky talk me into sharing a smoke on the patio. Although I wasn't really a smoker, never keeping a pack of my own, I would watch with anticipation as Ricky pulled his from a pocket in his coat and took out two .

cigarettes. I would reach for one and let it rest in my lips until he tendered a flame.

On a Monday afternoon, Teresa fired Ricky unexpectedly. This came after a weekend during which one of our baristas hosted a party in his apartment, inviting everybody from the café. I hadn't gone, but Ricky filled me in on the details. Sunday morning he had come into work hungover and late, saying he'd drunk a whole three-litre jug of someone's homemade wine the night before. He'd spent the entire night, he explained, sitting on the floor and playing a guitar, singing song after song.

And I guess I didn't notice I was drinking, he said. I didn't even get up all night, so I never had that moment when you try to stand and realize how really fucking drunk you are.

At some point in the night, Teresa arrived at the party, and after trying unsuccessfully to find her place amongst the crowd, wound up next to Ricky on the floor. She'd tried to get him into conversation, divulging the fact that she too was a lyricist, and had herself written a handful of songs. Getting nothing out of Ricky in response, she switched tactics and asked instead about the café. It being Saturday, she hadn't been in the kitchen for a couple of days. She told Ricky she worried about the café when she wasn't around to keep an eye on the place.

Whatever followed from there, Ricky couldn't remember. He told me he vaguely recalled having to defend me against something Teresa had said, and he thought that maybe things had got a bit heated. But, he assured me, it was nothing. He wasn't worried about it. For now, his only concern was how to get through this day without kicking the bucket.

I don't know how much help I'm going to be, he said while leaning into a counter, his elbows on the cutting board, his aching brain cradled into the futile comfort of his hands.

When he got fired, I was waiting for him on the patio. Ricky came out the side door, and without breaking his stride, announced he had been canned. I followed him across the street and into the park. He found a bench by the fountain, and we both sat down. Ricky lit a cigarette and described how Teresa had invited him into her office, and with evident restraint, informed him he wouldn't be working at the café anymore.

But didn't she give you any reason? I asked.

Not really, but I guess we must have had it out the other night. Apparently I said some things I shouldn't have said. Ricky blew a cloud of smoke into the air. Turning suddenly serious, he said, I don't drink very often anymore, but every time I do it seems like something bad comes out of it.

But you really don't remember what you said to her? I mean, nothing? None of it comes back to you?

Ricky said he must have been honest, that he must have spoken what we were thinking, all of us, all the time.

And that's what drives me crazy, he said. I don't regret what's happened, but it kills me to see so many people pissed off, and nobody says anything. It's dishonest. It's the worst kind of dishonesty, he said, when a person will not say what's on their mind.

I nodded, though I couldn't agree. In principle, sure, it sounded great, but what if you just didn't have the luxury? What Ricky doesn't realize, I thought, is that for some there is a forced calculation that goes into this.

Walking home later on, I felt sorry about what had happened. I felt sorry for Ricky, but I was envious too. Now that he'd been fired, I wanted to quit the café, but of course, I couldn't do that. After all, I had a family to support. But with Ricky gone, I wondered what the place would be like. I knew he wasn't the only one to have been recently fired from the café, but in a way this was different, this felt like an ending of sorts.

A couple days later, Teresa called me into her office to talk. Her office was in the basement, in a room that had been previously used for storage. Now it was cleared of all previous junk, and what remained was a handful of chairs and a fold-out table where Teresa worked. There were no windows, and the room reeked of cigarettes. It was dim and stale and gloomy.

She asked me to take a seat. On the table there was a computer with the monitor turned halfway toward me. On the screen, I could see my coworkers in real time, unwittingly captured on camera as they walked back and forth upstairs, behind the bar, fixing drinks and taking payments. In the background, I could even see into the empty kitchen where I should have otherwise been standing.

The first thing I want to tell you, Teresa began, is that you have nothing to worry about. I know there's been a lot of… there's been a lot of change recently, but I want you to know that you can rest assured. You're a hard worker, and I think you can be trusted. That's why I wanted to talk with you, that's why I asked you to sit with me here, because I think that we can work together, don't you?

At that moment, Teresa glanced toward the monitor where my co-worker Michel could be seen standing with his back to the register while a customer made awkward attempts to gain his attention.

I just need you to tell me that you're on board, Teresa said.

Of course I'm on board, I told her.

Great. That's terrific. In that case, I want to tell you about the chef I'm bringing in to replace Ricky on the weekend shift.

My heart sank.

This guy is a professional. I've known him for years, Teresa said. He's a great guy, the pick of the litter, and the very first person I thought to call. And it just so happens he's available! How lucky is that? I mean, this is someone who knows this business inside out and upside down. Someone who's going to be able to whip the rest of us into shape.

Teresa was wearing a big, dumb grin on her face. Meanwhile, with every word she spoke, I sunk deeper into despondency. I struggled not to react. The pick of *her* litter? Like a special recruit? Someone to come and whip us into shape? My god.

She went on: This is not someone who's going to come into work hungover. He doesn't even smoke.

Here she made a gesture of holding an invisible joint to her puckered lips.

I'm telling you David, she said, you'll be impressed.

Next, Teresa spoke of what she wanted from me. It was going to be my job to be like a sponge, she said. She repeated this same unsavoury metaphor several more times. I was to try and learn from him as much as I could. I was to stick with him and to soak up the wealth of his knowledge, just like a sponge.

When Teresa asked if she had made herself clear, I told her things were perfectly clear. When she asked if I was capable and willing to do what was needed, I told her I was.

I'll do it. I'll be like a sponge, I said.

I figured it didn't matter anymore what I did or didn't say. In the space of some weeks, my position within the café had been summarily altered. Still more, I felt as if my position in life had been taken away. For months I'd been thinking of myself as a cook, but the truth is I wasn't a cook. I'd never been one before and was not one now. I had become something else instead.

And if in the interim between then and now it had seemed a real possibility, if for these months I had entertained the idea that I could be a cook, that I might be a cook, well, best to consider it a failed experiment, an illusion circumstantially perpetuated for a season or two wherein I had briefly forgotten myself. To put it simply, I would never let this happen again. From now on, this job would be like every other job I'd had before: nothing but a means to earn a wage, nothing but a gross inconvenience dropped into an otherwise fine and decent existence.

I was a writer then, same as now, perennially occupied with other things. Back then I had so many stories in my head, same as I do now. I used to worry they would never be written because to do them properly, I knew, required something that I couldn't afford. I needed time, yes, but also more than that. I needed the kind of time that exists all around and throughout common time—that time which lifts individual moments and explodes them into infinity.

I was always tired and distracted then, and it was hard not to get discouraged. To be holding these stories was like holding a bouquet of wild and wonderful flowers no one could see. My whole sense of self-worth and confidence was wrapped in these dreams I couldn't make real.

At that time, there was one in particular, one among all those stories that I wanted to write. That was my war story, and I thought about it constantly. Even during that meeting with Teresa, sitting in her office as I handed myself away, even then I was thinking about it. I was feeling the weight and the hope of it with me.

The idea for that story came after I'd cut off the tip of my finger at work a few weeks before Ricky got fired. It happened around noon one day while I was working alone and the café was bustling. We were running out of food in the display case so I was making sandwiches to order while also trying to make a soup and replenish our stock of salads. At one point, I was roughly chopping a pile of mushrooms when I let my free hand get too close. As soon as the blade came down I felt a rush of pain like an electric shock from my hand, up my arm and into my the shoulder.

I dropped the knife. I knew right away that the cut was deep, so I went to the sink. I ran the tap and allowed the water to wash away the blood, but the bleeding wouldn't stop. It was still so busy in the café that I needed to get back to work. Of course, those mushrooms would need to be thrown away. *The cutting board and knife*, I thought, *will need to be washed*. As for what to do with my finger, I decided for the time being just to wrap it in some paper towel.

Later on, when things had quieted down, I went back to the sink to try and deal with my finger. By now it had been encased in a wad of brown paper towel for an hour or so, and when I tried to unwrap it, I found that the paper towel was stuck. I tried pulling against the resistance I met, but then I was hit with such a sudden force of pain that I had to stop. I had to take a breath. I tried wetting the paper towel, hoping to unglue it, but I couldn't bring myself to try unwrapping it again. My stomach buckled at the prospect. Feeling unable now to inspect or even clean my wound, I decided to wrap the whole thing up in a layer of gauze. Finger, paper towel, blood and water, all wrapped in gauze and tied together with some surgical tape.

I should have dealt with it after work, but my wife and I had plans to visit with some of her relatives that night. Cousin of an auntie's husband, I think, and that cousin's own husband, their kids and grandkids. They all lived out at Sainte-Anne de

Bellevue, so we would need to take a train just to get there, and by the time I was home from work we were already late. I was hardly able to get showered and dressed before we had to run out for the metro. And late that evening, coming home, after having been plied all night with food and wine, we fell straight into bed. So it wasn't until I was back the next morning at the café that I got to look at my wound.

I set myself up in the basement over a utility sink. All around me were rows of basic shelves we used to store our non-perishables. There was a bare light hanging overhead which made this all seem like an improvised surgery. By the sink I had a pair of scissors, a bowl of salt and some fresh bandages.

First I cut into the gauze and peeled away the outer layers of yesterday's paper towel. I found that everything was still a bit wet, a little bit sodden, and not only that, but I found that it had started to stink. And that was what did it, it was that smell. Although I had never encountered it, I knew right away what it was, as if by some animal instinct, I knew that this was the smell my blood left out overnight, that a part of my body had started to turn. For a moment I stood in a kind of awe, just considering the strangeness of the fact.

It must be something common in the human experience to have encountered this smell and yet it is an aspect of our existence which we have managed somehow to keep hidden away. Gangrenous limbs are said to stink, I thought, and what about the so many wounded in war? I began to imagine how a cut like this, one that was fairly minor, insignificant really, if suffered in the trenches, say of the First World War, could have been the death of someone. Just this, I thought, hardly more than a scratch. And then, there are likely places still in the world where a simple scratch could lead one to death, just for lack of access to things like clean running water, a sink, fresh bandages and a bowlful of salt.

Back upstairs, I was roasting a squash. By the time I'd finished in the basement, it was ready to come out of the oven. Later, when the squash had cooled, I set to work pulling the meat out of its skins. It was a butternut squash, and while I worked, the smell of that squash rose into the air and surrounded me. My plan was to make a soup.

Once again, I was struck by that smell. I mean, it wasn't the very same smell, but it was close enough. There was a definite similarity in it. So once again, I stood in a moment of something like reverie and tried to make sense of my thoughts. The fact that a roasted butternut squash could remind me of the smell of my own rotten blood seemed at least curious enough that I ought to write it down. I didn't know why I was writing it down, but that sort of thing, you don't just throw it away. Maybe I could use it somewhere, someday, I thought.

I called it a reminder of war. I imagined that for a person who had become say traumatically familiar with the smell of a rotten wound, how someday in their future they might be returned to their memories, triggered maybe at a family gathering when old aunt so-and-so brings out the pumpkin pie. Of course, I had never been to war and I didn't know anybody who had, but over the next few days this notion grew in my thoughts. I collected other so-called reminders of war. The retort of an egg cracked into a pan, the flash of sputtering grease, even the taste of something eaten off a slightly rusted, cast-iron dish. Of course, I had no reason to write about war. Only, I liked the idea of writing something entirely fictitious for once, something utterly different from all the loosely autobiographical stuff I had written before. Maybe it came from feeling stuck in the café, looking for a kind of escape.

I dug into my war story, which started coming together, if in an uneven way. From a collection of observations to an amassing of aesthetic details. The city in the 1920s. All red brick, iron, rolling river, fog and smoke. Some half-cocked veteran working as a cook. Greasyspoon, eggs and bacon, cup of coffee costs a nickel, all that. As I said before, I thought about it constantly, to the point of distraction. I kept writing things down. At work, every fifteen minutes or so, whenever I was struck with another idea, I stopped what I was doing and wrote it down.

Teresa had given us notebooks, one to every cook at the café. She said that if we were going to be working here, we should always be on the lookout for new ideas. We should be trying new foods and taking notes, finding recipes and writing them down. We should be vigilant, she said, and inspired. And if one truly wanted to be a cook, I suppose that is what they'd want to do. But I was filling my notebook up with ideas of an entirely different kind.

The new guy's name was Rob. He started work the following Saturday. At seven o'clock I saw him standing at a distance on the sidewalk. He looked to be in his mid-thirties and was wearing a bomber jacket and a baseball hat. At first he looked shady to me, actually. There seemed to be a shadow set around his eyes. I thought he looked like a disaster, but by then I was so tired of everything, it made no difference what I thought. I could barely even stand to introduce myself, I had so little left to give. Nevertheless, it was my job this morning to show him the ropes. Teresa told me I wouldn't need to train him. Professional that he was, she'd said, he would know just what to do. He'll jump right in, she'd assured me.

From the moment I opened the doors, as we stepped into the café, Rob launched an inquiry into every aspect of our work. He was as meticulous as he was scattered, asking about our inventory system, for instance, wanting to know what day we ordered our stocks and who was in charge of the task, and who, upon delivery of the goods, was responsible for signing waybills and receipts and where, finally, was the paperwork kept? With his very next breath, he was on about our baked goods wondering how many muffins we sold in a day and did we make the batter for these ourselves or did we use a prepackaged mixture? And if we did make the batter ourselves, how much sugar did we use? How much salt?

All of this caught me off guard and left me feeling badgered. First by questions, then by corrections. According to Rob, everything we did could be done in another way. And though not necessarily a *better* way, certainly a different way. Rob couldn't dice an onion without first asking what method we used. When I told him that we didn't have a method, that he could cut an onion any way he wanted to, he took it to mean that we hadn't given the matter any true consideration. He explained that there were many different ways to cut an onion, that a choice had to be made, and if you were looking for, striving for consistency, then the outcome of that choice ought then to be followed assiduously, by every member of our team.

It was only eight o'clock, but I felt like I was burning out. I went to make myself a cup of coffee. As a gesture, I offered to get one for Rob. Rob said he'd like a macchiato, and I had to admit I didn't know what that was. He explained that a macchiato was a shot of espresso with some frothy milk.

But only very little milk, he said. And the milk should be only lightly steamed.

I nodded, thinking it sounded pretty standard. When I handed him his coffee though, Rob took a small sip and shook his head.

Tell me how you made this, he said.

Without waiting for any answer, he went on to describe, in detail, the process of pouring a proper shot of espresso.

The trick was to let the first few drops fall. These were so full of bitterness, Rob explained, that they irritate not only your sense of taste, but also the process of the body's digestion.

A little later, Rob asked if he could step out for a cigarette. I practically insisted he should, thinking that I might finally have a moment of peace. He went out the side door onto the patio, but not half a minute later the door opened again and he was coming back in. He hung up his coat, washed his hands, and appeared to be ready to get back to work.

It was cold out there? I asked.

A little, he said, but not too bad.

I looked at the door. I looked at his coat hanging up on the wall, and then back at him. You can't possibly have just smoked a whole cigarette, I said.

Rob smiled. He fished in his pocket and pulled out a cigarette that had evidentially been lit, partially smoked and butted out.

I only ever take a couple of drags. When I'm at work, he said, it saves time and it keeps me on my toes.

Jesus, I said. That isn't natural. I mean, don't worry about it, please. Smoke a whole cigarette. It's still early, I assured him. We've got plenty of time.

Rob shook his head. I've been in this business for fifteen years, he said, and if there's one thing I've learned it's that there is never enough time to smoke a whole cigarette. Not now, he said, not ever.

The next morning Rob and I got into an argument after he accused me of being late. His position was that I should have been at the café at least ten minutes prior to the start of our shift. My position was one of disbelief. I couldn't believe that we were having this conversation, especially since it was only his second day on the job. Besides, as I pointed out to him, there were still a few minutes left before my shift. Rob wasn't convinced. He told me it was unprofessional, disrespectful.

I've been standing here for fifteen minutes, he complained, freezing my ass off in the cold, waiting for you.

Why would you show up fifteen minutes early and expect me to be here? I asked.

Once we were in the kitchen, we settled into separate tasks. The morning progressed, and then just before eight o'clock, Françoise arrived. After wishing us each a good morning, she asked if either one of us would care for a coffee. Rob said that he'd like a macchiato.

Avec plaisir, Françoise responded.

When he took a sip of his coffee though, Rob confided to me that it wasn't very good.

I'm going to have to have a talk with her, he said. I'll have to teach her how to pour a proper shot.

By nine we had settled into cooking for lunch. There were now two baristas working the bar, and Elizabeth was in, washing dishes in the back.

Liz was Ricky's girlfriend. She was tall, quite thin, and had willowy limbs. She was an Albertan originally, which was where she and Ricky had met, and where they'd started living together before reaching a decision to come to Montreal. Understandably, Liz was annoyed when Ricky lost his job. She told me that Ricky was stubborn, and describing the night of the party, she said she had tried to get Ricky to leave, and that she herself had gone home at a reasonable hour having drunk only a reasonable amount.

But you can't tell Ricky anything, she said. Not once he's in a certain mood.

At one point in the morning, while Rob was on an errand to the storage room, Liz took me aside and told me that Vincent and Val had been in the café last night, and that they had found a pile of empty beer bottles stashed in the walk-in fridge. They suspected that Rob had been stealing beers and drinking them while on the job.

From that point on, I started watching more carefully, and I did notice how often Rob would find an excuse to go into the walk-in fridge. I went in there myself a few times, and while nosing around I found an open bottle hidden in a case of purple onions. I noted the level of beer in the bottle and came back to check on it periodically. I guessed that by lunch Rob had drunk maybe three or four beers, and still he found new reasons to excuse himself into the fridge.

Well, I thought, *so what if he's been drinking on the job? So what if he's a thief, a bum and a drunk?* If anything, I was glad. Here was someone who had been hand-picked, who had been recommended to us as a model chef, as someone for us to emulate. Teresa had practically sold this guy as a prince, and so surely this would reflect badly on her. Maybe Vincent and Val would have a moment of doubt, a moment to reconsider the vote of total confidence that they had given her.

As Rob continued to drink, he became less of a nuisance to me. He started loosening up. He wasn't so focused on the work anymore. He even started telling jokes, and though they were awful—unbelievably abysmal puns for instance that felt forced and fell flat—it was an improvement. What was more, he started taking longer breaks. Once he stepped outside to smoke and was gone for over twenty minutes. There was a moment, then, wherein I was standing at my cutting board and the light of the afternoon splayed across the counter from a window above, and just for that moment, everything seemed calm, peaceful, set above the fray.

When the door finally pushed open and Rob came in, I said, You seem to be enjoying those more.

He laughed. I enjoy them, that's the problem, he said. I enjoy them too much for my own good. I'm always trying to cut back. It used to be that I was smoking five packs every day. I was working two jobs, fourteen-hour shifts, and for what? He turned suddenly serious and held up his pack of Du Mauriers. Just to pay for these godawful things.

That night I had plans to go with Ricky and Liz to see a show on Avenue Papineau. It was to be the first time outside of work that I'd be with them as friends. The band was one of Ricky's favourites. Several weeks before, when he'd heard they'd be playing a show, he immediately purchased three tickets without even asking me if I wanted to go. I hadn't been out very much since my son had been born, so that, combined with the fact that I'd never been out with Ricky and Liz, had me feeling both excited and nervous.

Our plan was to get to the venue by bike. Ricky and Liz came by the apartment early in the evening to pick me up. When they got there my wife had just run out to the depanneur, so we weren't able to leave right away. Ricky and Liz came to the top of our stairs and stood in the doorway. I stood in the hallway, holding my son. Since none of us seemed to know what to say, we stood there in silence for a full minute or two. Finally Liz remarked how after all this time, she'd never seen me with my baby. Ricky nodded.

You look good with a kid, said Liz.

I could tell they had already started drinking. Something in the way they stood on the fringe of our apartment, not sure of what to do with themselves. It was like they were afraid of a misstep, of stumbling or upsetting something if they came in. Soon though, my wife was home, and shortly after that we set off on our bikes. The venue was in a neighbourhood that none of us knew, but being pragmatic, Liz had studied a map of the area before leaving home and planned out a route for us to take.

She and Ricky were like opposites. He was all about passion and wanting to be lost. He wanted to be surrounded by music and didn't care much about anything else. Liz, for her part, had started taking classes at a college in her spare time. She was studying commerce and accounting. Four months before, when she had started working at the café, she'd been hired to wash dishes because she couldn't speak any French. Now she was still washing dishes, but she was also involved somehow in the general accounting of the business, managing our payroll among other things.

Liz had told me once that she was passionate about accounting. She loved numbers and their verifiability. Ricky sometimes made fun of her, referring to her as either his accountant or his personal manager. If she was his manager though, she didn't seem to hold too much sway over him. On our way to the show, Ricky sped off, keeping himself about half a block ahead of us all the way there. At first Liz and I tried to keep up, but soon found we couldn't manage his pace. We kept an eye on him though, watched him duck and weave, ride in and out of traffic, moving all over the road, senselessly, inattentively, even occasionally moving up onto the sidewalk.

Jesus, Liz muttered. She tried calling to him, but Ricky was too far ahead. He's like this every time he gets excited, she told me. And I don't want to be the one reining him in, but I swear someday he's going to get himself killed.

After parking our bikes, we stopped at a depanneur to pick up several tall cans of beer and took these to a park around the corner to sit, drink and smoke. We smoked a joint as well, and then lingered, telling stories in the cold. Ricky talked at length about the band we were going to see.

What they were known for, he said, was the depth of their sound. The production on each of their records was highly technical, experimental. They created, like a lacework of sound. Only no, he said, lace wasn't the right word. Lace was too delicate. It was more like a landscape, he said, with parts of it melded, blended together, as if it had been done with paints.

Liz was listening too, but it was clear that Ricky was talking to me. I began to wonder about this dynamic that had grown between us. It seemed like Ricky was always trying to teach me something. Whether it was him bringing new music into the café when we'd been working together, or addressing these explanatory monologues to me, it felt like he was always trying to expand my horizons. How he'd harp on about some album or artist made me wonder: Did he think I had no taste, no preferences of my own? I felt as if he was constantly trying to fill me up with what he figured would be valuable to me. Maybe I was being overly sensitive, but these days it was as if every new person in my life wanted to shape me into something. What was I doing to give off this impression that I was but an empty receptacle, waiting to be filled?

After drinking in the park, we crossed over to the venue, an old, baroque theatre that had at some point been renovated to accommodate a standing crowd. There were two bars serving drinks in the room, and as soon as we arrived, Ricky went off to order us a round. The show hadn't even started yet, and already I was feeling drunk. I reluctantly accepted a beer from Ricky, but then decided I was going to have to stop drinking. I went to the bar and ordered myself a soda water. I tried to buy a round of beer for Liz and Ricky, but for some reason Ricky didn't want to accept. In something resembling a vaudeville routine, he went back again to the bar for a beer, maybe thinking this would pressure me to drink the one I'd gotten for him, but I didn't give in. In the end, Ricky wound up drinking both of them.

We got stoned again after the opening act, and then Ricky disappeared for a while. I stood with Liz by the front of the stage while she danced to the intermission music. She looked happy and was glassy-eyed. She seemed to be off in a world of her own. At one point, she leaned in to tell me that it had been a year tonight since the last time she had taken cocaine.

You and Ricky? I didn't know you were into that.

Usually we aren't, but when we are… she said, trailing off.

She told me a confused story about one of their first nights in Montreal, something about an overweight man, their connection, and a narrow set of stairs into a loft. After that she laughed and went back to dancing alone.

I watched as she moved across the floor, coming close then going farther away. Somehow I'm missing something, I thought. I don't know who I am anymore, I don't know who I'm with and I don't know where we are or what we're doing here.

Ricky reappeared carrying two plastic cups, evidently from

the bar. As he approached, I saw that they were filled with an amber-coloured liquid.

It's Scotch. That's a fifteen-dollar shot, he said pushing one of the cups into my hands.

But I don't want this, I said.

Don't waste it, he chided.

It's too much money. Aren't you unemployed?

Ricky rolled his eyes. Take it up with my accountant, he said.

The next thing I knew, the lights went down and the band took the stage. Ricky turned with wide-eyed attention, and I followed his lead.

All in all, the band played for an hour and a half without breaking. There weren't even any breaks between their songs, but they did use all kinds of effects, layering and looping things, so that it was like one song never ended, but instead went on progressing, changing and coming apart. New songs would take shape out of the old ones, as if formed of the same material. The result was an accumulation of sound, it was sound as material, sound as mass. The effect was hypnotizing. You could get lost in a sound like that.

And part of me wanted to get lost. Part of me wanted to submit to the music, to submit to this night and get carried away. But still I didn't drink any of the Scotch, though I held onto the cup until the liquor warmed. I even lifted it up to my lips several times, but I only breathed it in. After a while I got tired of holding it, so when I thought that Ricky wasn't looking, I put it on a nearby table and left it there. Not twenty minutes later though, Ricky was handing me another cup.

This one, he said, was twenty-five dollars.

You're wasting your money, I told him. You know I'm not drinking this.

Liz came over when she saw what was happening. She didn't say anything, but she shook her head. I gave her a questioning look and she shrugged.

Ricky turned his attention back to the band. He was obviously bent on getting drunk. I had to admit I had been there myself, and though I hated to make him do it alone, I had my own life to think about. I put that second cup down on the same table as I had the first one. Another twenty minutes later, Ricky was back with another two drinks.

These are doubles, sixty dollars each, he said. That's the most expensive shit they've got, so drink it up and enjoy it.

By now, he was bleary, and whether or not I was drinking with him couldn't make any difference. Liz yelled something in his ear, but over the music I couldn't make out what it was. He didn't respond. He just stood there wearing a sideways grin, keeping his eyes on the stage. Liz shrugged and went back to dancing, but I went on watching him. Ricky looked almost victorious, proud in some way as he lifted his cup. The music at this point was thick and loud. Ricky was transfixed. He stood there, eyes on the stage, gulping his Scotch as the music played on.

After the show, our plan was to smoke some more pot for the bike ride home. Ricky stepped out of the theatre, and I was right behind him. He stepped over the curb, but I told him to wait.

Where's Liz? I asked.

Ricky turned around. She's standing right behind you, he said.

As he turned to cross the road, a van sped by and it clipped him with its side-view mirror. It happened fast and was surreal as Ricky was thrown sideways, hitting a parked car. He was bounced against the van again before he finally hit the ground.

Liz and I ran to him immediately. He was unconscious and laid out on his back. There was blood on the road, but it was hard to see where it had come from. There wasn't much of it, only a sort of patina spilled over the asphalt.

A crowd gathered out in front of the theatre, and a young man came forward who displayed such a level of confidence that he inspired our trust. He quickly took charge of the situation, instructing his girlfriend to dial 911. He pulled some other fellow out of the crowd and had him kneel next to Ricky with instructions to support his neck, and not to let him move his head, his neck, his arms or legs.

As we waited for the ambulance, Ricky regained consciousness but then it faded again. This happened a handful of times, and whenever he came to, Ricky would try to sit up, so that fellow from the crowd had to continually pin him down. I helped as well by keeping my hands on his chest. Every time Ricky tried to sit, we had to push to keep him laid out on the ground. Liz tried to discover where the blood was coming from. I kept glancing at her, expecting maybe hysterics, expecting at least for her to be in dismay, but I found her to be strangely calm. It was as if she were trying to figure out the source of the blood not so much for the sake of Ricky's well-being, but to satisfy her own curiosity. Of course, I knew she must be worried, but she kept telling me that this was just like the skiing accident Ricky had suffered while they had been back in Alberta. She said she'd seen him come out of worse than this.

When the paramedics arrived, they strapped Ricky to a board and loaded him into an ambulance. Apparently he had smacked his head against the road and they needed to take him to the hospital. There was only room for one in the ambulance, so Liz hopped in. I told her I would follow on my bike. After asking where they would be taking him, I left the scene and crossed the road to where we had parked our bikes. Leaving Ricky and Liz's bikes on the rack, I headed west toward Mount Royal. The paramedic had said the hospital would be on the mountain, so that's where I went. Eventually the ambulance caught up with me, and in an eerily quiet blaze of lights it fired past, blending into the city's distance.

When I got to the hospital I couldn't find the entrance to Emergency. I couldn't see any ambulances or any activity. Through the front doors, there was no one at the main reception desk. There was no one milling, fretting or sleeping in chairs. In fact, everything was quiet, the lights were low, and the building seemed almost abandoned. I followed a wide corridor, past the shuttered gift shop and a closed café, and then turned onto a smaller hallway, all the while looking for a person or an obvious sign of life. The deeper I went, the more empty the building seemed to be. Passing through secondary hallways now, all dimly lit and full of unmarked doors, I thought I could forget what I was looking for and still feel compelled to keep going, but it was only an errant thought. The truth is, I was still deeply embroiled in the practical matter of finding my friend.

While wandering, I met an old man who was doing more or less the same as me. He was wearing a heavy coat and looked to be about seventy years old. Speaking in French, he explained that he was looking for his nephew who had been admitted here. The old man didn't know where the nephew was, and like me, had been wandering the hospital. Together we found a bank of elevators and decided to move onto the second floor. The old man waited inside the lift and held the doors as I had a look around. Finding nothing on the second floor, we moved up to the third, the fourth, the fifth. On every new floor it was the same routine. The old man stayed back and held the doors as I walked for some distance into the darkness. Back in the elevator, we would carry out a debriefing about whatever I had found, which was invariably nothing. As the doors shut we would see ourselves reflected in the sheet-metal panelling. At one point, the old man started laughing, so then I started laughing too. Then he started crying, but I kept on laughing doggedly, persistently. Eventually the old man gave in and we were both laughing again, riding from the fifth to the sixth, and so on.

Somewhere in the midst of all this we found a nurse, or maybe he was some sort of night clerk. At any rate, this hulking figure wearing hospital scrubs had access to a nearby computer and was able to tell me that Richard Pistales was in an altogether different hospital. Apparently there was a second hospital on the mountain, one I hadn't known about. Ricky, said the nurse or clerk, was at Montreal General, farther down the road.

How much farther? I asked.

The nurse clerk guessed it was a mile or so.

By the time I got to him, Ricky had been admitted into Primary Care. He'd been given a bed in a large room full of patients, each with their own similar bed on wheels so that they could be shuffled around easily. There were nurses swarming in and between everyone, both omnipresent and inconspicuous.

Liz was sitting next to Ricky's bed. She was handling a scrap of wool from the sweater he'd been wearing, which the paramedics had cut off of him. Liz was quietly turning the scrap of wool back and forth in her hands.

It's such a shame, she was saying. This was the nicest piece of clothing you owned.

Ricky, now awake and with his neck in a brace, was strapped to the bed with a stack of monitors over his shoulder. There were wires running between his body and the monitors, and an IV needled into his arm. Ricky didn't know what was happening and every now and then he would ask us, so Liz and I would need to explain that he was in the hospital. We would need to explain to him why he was here, and every time we repeated the fact that he'd been hit by a van, he became frightened. Then his fright would transform into incredulity. It was as if he thought we were making it up. The trouble was that he had taken a serious blow to the back of his head, and besides that, he was drunk, so he was also disoriented. He couldn't remember the accident, nor could he retain the information that Liz and I tried and tried to impart.

Let's get out of here, said Ricky to Liz. I feel like shit, but really I'm fine, he pleaded with her. Come on Lizzy, let's go. Take me home, he practically begged.

Liz maintained her composure. Babe, she said, we have to wait until the doctor can X-ray your brain.

She pointed out to me that Ricky was angry, which had to be taken as a positive sign. His anger, she said, shows that he's himself.

Ricky complained he was thirsty, so we signalled a nurse who brought him some water in a small paper cup. When Ricky tried to drink, he felt sick. It looked like he was going to vomit, so Liz held up a garbage can, but because of his brace and the straps holding him down, Ricky couldn't turn to the side and he wound up spewing all over the front of himself. At the same time, some of those monitors over his shoulder went into alarm. Suddenly there were nurses rushing in, and because there wasn't enough room around the bed, I was pushed aside, which was fine by me. Seeing Ricky like that made my own stomach turn. My face felt hot and my neck was flushed.

I found a sink in the middle of the room where I wet a paper towel and applied it to the back of my neck. Hospitals sometimes had this effect on me. I felt light-headed, as if I might lose consciousness. Where I was standing, I was surrounded by people in beds, all with wires, tubes and needles disappearing into them, hidden under their gowns. There was something unnatural about it, something so abstract. The body was at the very centre of everything that happened in this place—the body injured, suffering and broken down—and yet in the process of it being mended, the body was completely debased. It was this disconnect between process and intent that had me feeling so faint.

I thought about my war story. I tried to imagine a scene like this, a hospital in the field, set someplace five miles back from the front. The floors would be covered in stretchers, row on row, with men gruesomely injured, horribly wounded, disfigured, crying out in pain.

Across from me was a woman in bed. Nothing more than a fat, middle-aged woman lying under a sheet. One of her legs exposed, there was the shape of a purple bruise. She looked exhausted, but as if she couldn't sleep. Her arm was thrown up to cover her eyes, so I could even see the stubble of her armpit.

I looked at this woman and thought of my story. But how could any story measure up to the simple, honest fact of her— this woman, whose existence should mean nothing to me. How could any invented narrative ever stand up against the humble reality of this stranger-woman's stubbly armpit?

I spent another half hour at the hospital. For a while I ended up in a hallway just outside the main room that Ricky was in.

There were still more patients here in their wheeled beds, but it was quieter. The lights were low, and the people were mostly asleep. I spent some time studying an informational chart on the wall about head injuries. It mentioned symptoms attending to long term effects, spoke of problems, possible complications and warning signs that one should look out for. By now it was well after two o'clock in the morning and I wasn't sure there was much I could do hanging around the hospital. Ricky had been given a sedative, so he was sleeping. Liz was sitting by the side of his bed. When I told her I'd decided to leave, she offered to walk me out, but first she reached into the pocket of Ricky's jeans, slung over the back of the chair, and extracted his pack of cigarettes.

Together we walked to the edge of a parking lot where I had locked my bike. We sat on a concrete divider and smoked. There wasn't much for us to say. Everything seemed obvious and trite. In lieu of anything else, Liz and I ended up talking about the café. It was a boring, tedious conversation, but I think it did both of us some good just to sit and talk and share a smoke.

I was off work for the next two days. My son had started waking up early, sometimes as early as five o'clock. I got out of bed with him, and because it was hard to stay awake sitting around the apartment, I bundled us up against the cold, and wearing him in an infant carrier, took us out for a walk. Recently he and I had discovered that besides the all-night diners on Rue Notre-Dame, besides the neighbourhood strip club which seemed never to close, the only place open early nearby was the Atwater Market building. The shops and the market stalls themselves wouldn't open up for another hour or so, but the building itself was a place to keep warm, so on those early mornings we walked to the market, crossing the barren fields and the railroad tracks. We waited and watched as the shops opened up. First the butchers and the bakeries, and then finally the small café at the end of the row where I could get a coffee before walking us home.

During those days I had no news of Ricky. I thought about visiting the hospital, but then decided against it. Aside from an illogical suspicion that I might not be able to find the building again, I just figured that it wasn't my place. I was neither family, nor a close friend. In fact, I realized I didn't even have a phone number for Ricky or Liz, because until now, I'd never needed one. I couldn't even be sure if Ricky was still in the hospital. And if he was, I didn't know if he would want to be seen.

By Wednesday I was back at work. First thing in the morning, Teresa called me into her office and asked why I hadn't come to her to tell her about Rob.

Here we had someone stealing from us and drinking on the job, Teresa said. It was your responsibility to keep me informed about something like that, she explained. How am I supposed to do my job if you can't be trusted to do yours? she asked.

A slew of defensive statements, of objections and qualifications, got caught and mixed up on the way to my mouth. In the end, I just loudly exhaled. After all, what was the point of trying to fight back? She had already won.

Why did you tell me he didn't drink? was all I could finally manage to ask.

I never said that, Teresa snapped. What I said was that he didn't even smoke.

Later, while we were working in the kitchen together, Teresa decided to tell me about the last time she hired Rob for a catering job. It was sometime last year, and she'd given him a simple list of dishes he was supposed to have prepared.

She'd even trusted him enough to send her clients to pick up the food. So this husband and wife whose daughter was about to be married showed up at his apartment, she said. And this was first thing in the morning, but they found him drunk. He opened his door to them in his underwear and none of the food had been made.

Even as she told me this story, Teresa was laughing. Well, I guess he does have a real problem with alcohol, she said. Go figure. It's just such a shame—he's such an excellent cook.

Before the end of that day, Liz came in to do an hour's worth of office work. She'd come from the hospital, she told me, and would be heading back that way immediately. Ricky still hadn't recovered much. She said his brain had been hemorrhaging, and that it had been swollen for days against the back of his skull.

Walking home from work, I thought about the words *hemorrhaging, swollen, brain* and *skull*. I tried to connect these words with the thought of my friend lying there in his hospital bed, but every time I came close, I mean every time I thought I could almost understand what those words meant, I began to feel sick. I could see Ricky as he had been at the time of the accident. His body thrown like an object, dashed defencelessly onto the road. The look on his face as he moved in and out of his consciousness. His confusion, his obvious pain.

I thought then that I would never do well in a war. I was too squeamish, too sensitive, too easily overwhelmed.

That weekend, I had to work with Rob again. By now everyone knew about his drinking, but we had no one to replace him with just yet. Teresa had instructed me to pretend as if I didn't know anything. She said Rob was going to come into work, and if he continued to drink, so be it. On Monday we would make a tally of however many beers had gone missing, and while firing Rob, Teresa would present him with a bill for whatever amount he owed.

On Saturday, Rob looked dishevelled. He came in fifteen minutes late and apologized, but I told him not to worry. He quietly set himself up with a task, and the morning progressed with us working separately, but side by side. At one point I overheard him talking with some of the baristas. He was standing by the espresso machine trying to explain to them how to pour a shot. I overheard the words bitterness and irritant, and I could see him trying to make a demonstration, but nobody was listening.

Throughout the morning he kept finding reasons to get into the walk-in fridge, and I found reasons to get in there after him. For me, it was just a curiosity, as I had no intention of reporting anything back to Teresa. By noon, I figured he had had six beers, and his mood had lightened considerably.

After the lunch rush, Liz came in to pick up a cheque. She stopped in the kitchen and told me that Ricky was doing much better now. He was still dizzy, had a headache and was suffering memory lapses, but all of that was beginning to fade. The doctors thought that in time, it was possible for him to make a full recovery. It seemed for now as if he was out of the woods.

I was relieved and felt a weight had been lifted. Liz went out the side door and as she did, the afternoon sun momentarily blazed into the kitchen, lighting up the counters, the food, the floors, the knives and the whites we were wearing. Rob had been standing next to me, so he heard everything that Liz had said, but he didn't know Ricky and he didn't know anything about the accident. Although he didn't ask, I felt compelled to tell him what had happened. I told him about the accident and its aftermath, I told him about the show, about the band, about the music. I told him about the hospital, and about having gone to the wrong hospital at first. I even told him about the old man who'd been looking for his nephew.

After I finished, I imagined there would be an awkward pause. After all, I couldn't really explain what had compelled me to tell the story at such a great length to Rob, but I didn't have time to wonder about it because without missing a beat, Rob launched into a story of his own. And for so many reasons it was clear that he was making this story up as he went along, or if maybe there was some kernel of truth within it, he was smothering that truth in embellishment.

Rob told me that the year before last, he had also been hit by a car. Only at the time, he'd been riding a bicycle. The car, he said, had immediately fled the scene, and Rob had had to get himself to the hospital alone. Nobody stopped to help, he said, although he was very clearly distressed: wounded, bleeding and dragging his heap of a bicycle along. At the hospital, he said, they had sent him home. They told him there weren't enough beds. They said all he needed was some rest, and so he went home and fell asleep on the couch.

When I woke up, I couldn't remember a thing. I didn't know what had happened, only that I was hurt so bad I couldn't get off my couch. I couldn't even get up, he said, to get myself a drink of water from the kitchen sink.

Rob said he spent three days wallowing and wasting away on his couch, and that he probably would have died if his boss at the time hadn't realized that something was wrong.

See, because I hadn't been in to work, and I hadn't even been able to make a phone call, because I couldn't even move to get to the phone and couldn't even remember that I *had* a job, well, my boss figured that something must be terribly wrong because I was otherwise so totally reliable, so he called the police. The cops showed and broke open the door, then seeing so much blood and debris, the officers pulled out their guns. And that's how they found me, said Rob. With their guns drawn, standing over his couch, asking him how this all had happened. And the thing was, I couldn't remember, he said. But anyway, those cops saved my life.

When Rob finished talking, I didn't know what to say. He went back to work, bending over his cutting board. I shook my head as if to clear it of a fog that had accumulated.

In another few minutes Rob would put down his knife. He would walk to the door and head outside to smoke. In another few days he would be fired. And then, coming in some time after that to collect what would be left of his pay, he would corner me and recount in a harsh, conspiratorial tone how he had been mistreated, how he had been abused, how Teresa had taken advantage of him.

A few months later I would lose my own job, but by then it wouldn't matter. It would be winter, there'd be snow on the ground. And later still, other seasons. Time would pass. Teresa would eventually run the café into the ground. There would be no more Riviera. No more heavy, early mornings. No more keys in pockets, nor light coming in at the window.

This fog, I thought, will lift and everything attending it will be dispersed.

THEN SHE SMILED AND WALKED AWAY

I've been working for this one construction company now for almost a year, and lately it seems my boss has been shaping me into his errand boy. It sounds bad, but I actually like running errands. It beats hauling concrete, say, climbing all day up a steep path with fifty-pound bags on your shoulder. It beats digging a hole, working in the rain, looking for a leak in a water line. Because that's the kind of work I have been doing otherwise, all of it much more strenuous, and more tiring than running errands. It's important to me that I am not overly tired at the end of the day, because at the end of the day, I don't have to work for anyone anymore so I like to have a little energy left to do the things I like to do. I like to read books, for instance. I like to lie back and think about things.

If I'm going to be running errands, what I might do is take

a truck home with me at the end of the day. The next morning I will get in the truck and drive to the local dump, to the auto parts store, and then to grab a coffee somewhere. After that it's to the lumberyard, the hardware store and the gas station. The company I work for operates out on an island, so we are always having to fill up about a hundred jerries with gasoline. Then I'll load them onto the truck and head to the local marina to meet our barge. We have our own barge which is used to carry our vehicles back and forth. A truck will leave the island loaded with junk, and it'll come back loaded with gasoline.

And what's funny about all this is when I have to park one of these trucks overnight on the road out front of my apartment building. Because the thing is huge and ghastly, with old toilets, water heaters and bags full of garbage just about overflowing in the back. People must see it and think, My god, what kind of an asshole drives a truck like that? They must form an image of that person in their minds, and what's funny is that I am not that person. I am young, a quasi-intellectual guy, fairly modest, quiet and slight. Most of my spare time is spent reading books and just thinking about things.

Really, most of my time I spend just trying to make sense of our existence. Because as far as I can tell, ours is an existence wherein not much of consequence happens. I mean, of course things happen along the way. We do bump into things now and then. But we also spend an awful lot of our lives just waiting and waiting, and I think that in fact we spend so much of our lives waiting for something to happen, that we begin to forget we are waiting, and we begin to believe that things are happening, when the truth is that, really, they're not.

Most of what happens is trivial, cultivated, funny little things to distract us. Like when a few weeks ago two guys from the company were drywalling somebody's house, and after they'd finished, our boss got a call from the clients to say that their cat was lost and they figured it was drywalled into the wall. The guys had to go back, help locate the cat, and cut into the wall to release it. Apparently they had boarded right over it. After that, of course, we all had a wicked laugh, but then we more or less forgot about it. And that's the kind of thing that's happening all the time. Good for a laugh, but quickly forgotten.

Recently though, something happened. It was around lunch one day, and I was at the marina waiting in the truck for the barge to come in. By the way, this is one of the best things about being an errand boy, how you can wind up with downtime throughout the day. Now I bring a book with me to work because I can often find time to read a page or two. Today I was reading one by Miriam Toews called *A Complicated Kindness*. For a minute though, I couldn't find the book in my knapsack and I wanted to bang my head against the steering wheel because I thought I'd forgotten it at home. That's one of the worst things that can happen, when you have an opportunity to read a book while being paid, but you find that you've forgotten it. Luckily though, I found it. It had been hiding near the bottom of my bag, partially hidden beneath the sandwich I packed for lunch.

I decided to take them both, book and sandwich, and find a place to sit outside, but first I went into the marina hoping for a cup of coffee. They serve a real swill in there, but it's cheap, costing only a buck. There's this table on the way to the washrooms with a hot plate and a coffee pot, cups and packets of sugar, but no cream. You're supposed to serve yourself. There's this box on the table with a slot, and that's where you're supposed to put your money. There's no one around, so the whole thing works on the honour system, but there's never any money in the box. I know because when I get curious, I pick up the box and shake it around. I'm probably one of a few people who ever really drinks coffee out of this place and that's because I'm young, I think. Or else stupid enough to enjoy an especially bad cup of coffee from time to time.

Anyway I was soon outside, reading my book, drinking my coffee, eating my sandwich and enjoying myself. There was a crowd of pigeons and seagulls around, going nuts watching me eat. They were trying to press in, trying to get close, so every now and then I had to kick up my legs and swing them in a gesture of violence. They would scatter after that, then settle further back, still watching as I went on eating.

At some point I looked up and noticed that a red hatchback had driven into the parking lot. A man was driving. He didn't park at first, but rolled around instead. Eventually he pulled in next to our company truck. I had parked the truck so that it faced the boat-launch ramp, so that when the barge came in, it would be ready to go. It was parked in one of those extra long spots meant to fit a truck with a boat trailer. Now this man in his comparatively little car pulled ahead, drove past the truck and turned around, and then started backing up toward the ramp. It looked as if he was going to descend the ramp, which of course would have taken him into the ocean.

At first I thought he was trying to imitate one of those trucks, the way they go backward down the ramp until their trailers run into the water. I had seen those big trucks doing it a hundred times by now myself. But that didn't make any sense. Of course he wasn't pretending to be a truck.

The car rolled back until it was on the ramp, but at this point there was some sort of a bush in the way, interrupting my line of sight. I didn't see the car go into the water, but I waited. I listened, but didn't hear anything. Maybe, I thought, the driver is just about to realize his mistake, and in a moment of embarrassment, he'll send his car flying up the ramp, speeding out of the parking lot. A few minutes passed, and nothing happened. I felt suddenly nervous, so I jumped to my feet and ran until I could see around the bush. Mysteriously, the car had disappeared. There was nothing on the ramp, and no sign of a disturbance in the water.

I was pacing, wondering now what to do. *I should tell somebody, but who? And what should I tell them?* I wondered. The office at the marina was closed as the staff had all gone out to lunch. I thought I ought to call someone. What was the number to call when you thought that maybe you had seen a car slip quietly, secretly into the ocean? And what about the driver? Was he dead? Was this a situation warranting emergency response?

I went back to what was left of my coffee. Surely in a moment I would know what to do. I thought about dialling information, but did people still use 411? For now, it was best to relax and wait for a better idea to come.

Nothing came, and soon I had waited so long that here was my boss pulling in with the barge. By now, I'd even started doubting myself. Had I really seen what I thought I had? Had I only imagined it? Had I somehow missed the car driving off when I wasn't looking, itself and its driver alive and intact?

My boss would never believe it if I told him what I thought I'd seen. I hardly was able to believe it myself. So, I didn't say anything. At least, not yet. I simply got into the truck, drove onto the barge, and as we pulled away, I stood on the deck and peered, searchingly, into the murky water.

That was a Friday afternoon, and there were lots of other things going on at work. There were jobs that had to be finished before we could pack it all in for the weekend.

Back on the island, I rejoined the crew. They were busy, some hauling bundles of shingles up a ladder, others hammering away at a roof. I joined them going up and down the ladder, and it was tiring work, so we took a lot of breaks. It was payday too, so everyone talked about how they were going to spend their money.

Lucas would be going to yet another show by yet another of his many favourite bands. Lucas is broke, but he's always spending eighty, ninety, a hundred dollars to see another one of these bands perform on stage. He's always complaining too, saying that he can't play guitar anymore like he used to do, not since his hands have become so hardened from work.

Jacob would be doing nothing tonight. Same as every other night. He never does anything. These days he's dating an inexplicably attractive girl, and as usual, they planned to spend the evening sitting on Jacob's living room couch, smoking pot and streaming pirated foreign films.

We asked John what his plans were, what he was doing with his weekend. John was the old guy, the carpenter. He said he'd be doing nothing too, but a different kind of nothing, looking after his mom. We nodded our heads. John's mother is dying, we all know that, but it's something so far removed from our own lives of youth and distraction that we often forget. She is dying slowly of old age and John has taken to living with her in a place way out beyond the edges of town. John told us that his was a life of nothingness, the likes of which we couldn't understand. When he said that, we all had to laugh. We couldn't help it. He said this to us all the time, like a broken record, over and over again.

Finally, the guys asked if I had any plans. I knew there was something I was meant to remember. It was something important, but my mind was a blank. I opened my mouth to start talking, hoping that whatever it was would come out. And it did.

Sylvie's got an opening, I said to them.

Sylvie is my girlfriend, and an artist. We've been together for over six months. Aside from being an artist, Sylvie works in a small café which I frequent for its excellent breakfasts, and because on the weekends it's a good place to sit, to read a book and to drink a cup of coffee. It's also a good place to read the news, and to drink five cups of coffee, if that's what you want. I mean, if that's the kind of day you want to have.

In her art, Sylvie uses only black and red ink. She draws with these pens that have a practically microscopic tip, and she creates intricate patterns of concentric, elliptical shapes, many overlaid onto each other, but all of shifting sizes and degrees. The effect is of something almost delicate, but also of tremendous internal tension. They are like headaches or knots tied into wood. Like a stomach cramp, or the shell of a nut.

One woman, reviewing Sylvie's last show, claimed that "the artist was unwittingly drawing the contents of her womb." She wrote this long, intellectual piece about the gesture of a young woman baring her womb on gallery walls. Sylvie, she said, was dumb both to the trappings, as well as to the potentials of her own femininity. Or, maybe she used the word "womanhood." Sylvie, she said, belonged to a new generation in which gender was largely repressed. Sylvie and I read the review together and laughed about it for an hour or more, but not because the woman's ideas were absurd, or even specifically untrue. It just seemed, more than anything else, that the writer was bored.

Now, as the afternoon was wearing on, the guys and I decided to quit taking so many breaks, to buck up and get those shingles onto the roof. And we did, though it very nearly killed us. We were sore and tired at the end of the day. I was so tired, in fact, that I had almost forgotten about the car.

Lots of people came out to the opening, and Sylvie was busy all night talking, trying to explain what could not be explained. Every so often she would lift her eyes, and looking across the gallery, finding me or another friend, would raise her eyebrows and make a face.

If I was going to tell anyone about the car now, it would need to be her, but we hardly had a chance to talk. Actually, I was alright with that. I didn't really feel like talking anyway. All night in fact, I felt morose. I was tired and sad, and because I was sad, I wound up drinking too much wine. It was supposed to be free for people on the guest list, but I guess I drank so much that the bartender wanted to cut me off. In the end, he didn't have the nerve. He only cut me off from the free stuff. After that I had to pay, but it didn't slow me down.

Being drunk, I figured, was fine as long as I could avoid too much talking. I didn't talk to anyone, all night long. Just about the only thing I said was goodbye to Sylvie, standing at the door. She wanted to go out with her friends and I wanted to go home, but I told her I'd be into the café for coffee sometime tomorrow morning. Before leaving, I congratulated her because it seemed everyone was excited about her art, and that made me happy for her, for what it was worth.

In the morning, I felt like death. I couldn't eat breakfast, so I headed out and went straight to Sylvie's café. I was in before she even arrived.

Sylvie came in looking bleary and a little worse for wear. She saw me sitting at a corner table and made a gesture as if to say, Sorry, but I'm already late. I'll come over to talk when I can. Then she stuck out her tongue and put on a look of exaggerated nausea. I widened my eyes and nodded as if to say, I'm right there with you.

Today was definitely going to be a five-cups-of-coffee type day. I'd already grabbed some newspaper from the pile on a table by the door. The papers had been picked apart, so what you got from the pile was a melee of sorts, different sections scrambled together, and often from different days of the week. At any rate, the news is always the same. The entire world is going to hell. We're on a sinking ship, and nobody cares. We've got days left, maybe weeks, maybe months.

On the front page of the provincial section, there were two stories that caught my attention. The first described how the government had started rewriting the Fisheries Act. Apparently all this protecting of fish was getting in the way of the economy so they wanted to weaken the definition of what could be called a "fish habitat." Poor fish, I thought. They don't even know. They can't even prepare for what's coming.

The other story was something curious about a woman in one of the northern towns. The woman was a widow but had recently become convinced that her husband was still alive. He was hiding in the mountains, she claimed, and had been doing so for years. Had been coming into town every two or three days to pick up groceries and other supplies. He was never any good at planning, she said, by way of explaining the frequency of his forays into town. Anyway, now the woman had publicly threatened to kill herself if he didn't come home.

The story cut off for me at that point, said to be continued on the ninth page. I looked for that page, but it was missing. That entire section of the paper had been pulled apart. I felt worried for a moment—worried for that woman and the whole situation. I thought there had to be some way for me to find out the rest of the story, and of course there was and it would have been easy, but already I'd begun to move on. In the next moment, my worry had passed. For all I was concerned, that woman might already be dead and it wouldn't make a lick of difference in my life.

I went to the counter and ordered a double espresso, long with a little milk. When it was ready, Sylvie brought it to the table. She also brought a rag so that she could stand and pretend to be wiping the table down.

I might not make it through the day, she said.

I know, I said. I feel the same way.

What happened to you? You didn't come out with us.

I was drinking at the gallery, I said. I had enough wine to take out a horse.

Sylvie laughed, and then she winced.

Hey, I wanted to tell you something, I said.

Tell me later. I've got to get back to work.

Do you want to get together later?

Maybe when I'm done, she said. We could try out that Thai place for dinner.

Sylvie had been trying for a while to get me to go to this new Thai restaurant. The problem was that it had opened in the place where another Thai restaurant had been before. The old restaurant had been awful so I naturally doubted that this new one would be good. I gave Sylvie a doubtful look.

I know, I know, she said. But I have a good feeling about it.

She leaned forward and almost gave me a kiss but didn't. Then she smiled and walked away.

THE NO—CRY
SLEEP SOLUTION

for the fish, and for the pond

Been a while now I've been talking with the ghost of an old friend—months of locked into nothingness, writing errant-headed phrases on a notepad by the bed. I complain.

That's the way it is, she says.

Of course, I say, and hang my coat over the back of a chair.

She asks me as I sit, Do you still see cursive patterns in the smoke of a cigarette? Or does this, like so many other notions, dissipate and fade over the years?

I tell her yes, but also no. I tell her I'm supposing violence, pretending actually, while proposing some good loneliness might come about by her.

Not in whatever smoke I'm breathing, I explain. What comes out of my lungs, over my own lips is utter gibberish.

I tell her how I could not have believed it would happen again, not after my son was born. What happened? The leaves turned yellow. And it seems to have happened all in a day.

How could the seasons go on changing? I said. That's what I caught myself thinking. Just as they had always done before...

They did, she said. They do.

Apparently.

And it means as much as anything else, she supposed, and my friend curled her long arm up to pull on her cigarette. Then she blew a cloud of dissipated words into the room.

A glass broke on the kitchen shelf. A pile of spoons fell to the floor. Somehow neither this nor that awoke the baby in his bassinette. When the water heater broke, we got used to carrying stones from the oven into the bath. You get used to everything, eventually. Everyone does.

This is how it happened, they say: the winds picked up, and they never let off.

I drew a bath one time in the late afternoon. I closed the bathroom door and turned on the light. At that time of day, the apartment was full of the long, low light of a dwindling sun. I spent such a long while in the tub, I believed that in the meantime the sun would have set. There were no windows in the room. The faucet dripped. I did nothing to correct it. I only gazed into the bare, white tiles of the wall in the bare white light of the overhead bulb. This is to say that when I opened the door, I expected to find myself entering a different apartment. I expected darkened rooms and the mood of a different time. Instead it was still light, the westerly rooms still cut with the long, low light of the sun. Same long sun as at the end of every day. I checked the clock to be sure this wasn't a dream.

I tell my friend, It was twenty-two minutes past five. So, I said to myself, fuck it, go to sleep. And sleep into evening, all night, until dawn.

➤⬤

She's in the bedroom with a man. He's got ten years on both of us, pepper on his body.

She's saying, Tell me what it was like before.

The man starts telling his story: Where I come from the people hung like marionettes. There were diners open all night, selling pizza and fries with gravy and a can of Coke for $3.25. Everyone paid what they could for what they needed. Whatever they didn't have, they couldn't afford. They needed love, they paid. And women had a habit of walking right into your house, right out of the rain, to dry themselves on your bedsheets. I come from a cruel place, an angry place, but also a simple place. When a woman left a man's house she'd leave his front door hanging open, and every man was either too lazy or tempered to shut it. So like mouths in the morning, as you walked down the street, you saw the gaping, empty mouths of doors saying who'd been here and who'd been there. Who had had some kind of money for love. Nobody slept well. In our town there should be no rainy days. There hadn't been a war in sixty-five years, so the people took it out on themselves. There was all kinds of violence. People walked into the river during the middle of the day. The streets were empty. People holed up in their rooms. They shredded their drapes with knives from their kitchen drawers.

When I left that place—this was years ago now—there was nothing to speak of in my life but a pile of wet clothes in the grass. One leaf overturned in the wind, as they say. We stood in the park, ragged, dirty and rained upon, burned but never changing in the flame of human sport. One pant leg cut into the middle thigh. Some would have said: My god, what a pity. Some would say: What a time we had.

So, I came to this place, where the people lived like crabs. Then seeing such a heap of abandoned spaces—factories, waterways, bridged and bricks—I crossed the street, wanting to meet someone there. I cried into a payphone, trying to make a call. And of course, my shoes got wet, as well as my belt and underpants. Finally, I looked up to see what was dripping, to find where the water was coming from. Over me was nothing but open sky and I realized it was only raining, again, after everything.

My friend lights a cigarette.

And I'm watching all this from under the covers of sleep. I tell my friend to tell the man that we're all in this together, but she doesn't hear, or doesn't want to talk.

My friend turns out the light.

The truth is that I have it better than so many people, better even than most. I've got a little hole to fit my family in. We keep six sharp knives in the kitchen drawer.

What's this noise about? My eyes caved in for listening. Ribs of the sidewalk, stutter to step. Cats into houseplants, get themselves off. I want more of this holiday—wait long for me on the coast.

What are these five hundred brilliant places? Where are our sails cut into the wind, forging vice versas over the great grey seas? My friend wore her black pants tight tonight and her shirt cut oh so low. I couldn't wave a hand in her silk, couldn't conceive of such words as a poet would say.

Forty-one hours. Forty-two days.

And I am not responding to anything. Somehow this has become a pastime for me—to scribble such words as these in sleep, in the morning, in the middle of the day. In every stolen moment. Turn one leaf—burning. And jets will put a storm into the sky.

I am a wreck, exhausted. I am under your spell. I've already hit myself off three times today, but I cannot shake the desire to be washed, to dry myself in your sheets. It's a mental thing. Neurotic, a kind of disorder I suppose.

I'm in pursuit of some mystery, where maybe there's none, but listen:

A body turns up on the side of the road, stuffed into a bush, by the old high school. A week later we'll have found his killer in the trash of so many wasted days. He says he thought he was his father so he cut him with a knife. He says he thought he was— not unlike the logic of a certain type of dream.

It's a kid who finds the body. Seventeen. Our detectives say they've never seen a corpse bleed out so much. Never seen a body that was once so full, now so emptied of its blood.

The kid says, I want a drink of water.

They give him a muffin and some cold caffeine. They give him a bench to sit or sleep on.

In the meantime, I've been carrying a pile of stones inside my pocket. When the kid finds the body, he's got a branch of yucca, held like a torch in his hands. All this raises a number of questions—wider and wilder than who, what and where.

Tonight, my friend is on her knees, praying, hands clasped, at the side of the bed. I'm at the desk killing flies. Rather, I am trying to kill flies, but for a while I can't manage it. They're too fast. I try again and again to catch them between the top of the desk and my palm. With practice, I am improving. Now I catch them under my hand and press, flattening every crevice of my palm into the desk, but every time I lift my hand, the fly flies away.

She's murmuring and I hear now and then supplications to the Virgin, to the Lamb and the Sky. To the intricate cosmos of the intractable soul.

I tell her I am certain that God is on a different channel by now. He doesn't respond to these traditional calls, I said.

She says, God is not affected by our changing notions of his being.

I purse my lips and nod. Is this the same girl who told me she was afraid of Jesus Christ?

Oh, she says, Christ I cannot fathom. With Christ, I am appalled. He's fit for bushes, nexus, wilderness and an overly protracted youth. I mean, the light, the truth and the way? Not to mention the law—give me a break.

She says, I've been doing this for twenty-two years myself. So tell me, what business has Christ in mine?

She spits and goes back to her prayer.

I swat a fly on the desk and it lives another fifteen days.

I ask her, Listen, have you got anything to drink? My heart doesn't seem to be beating right.

I broke all my bottles, she says. I got drunk and then I got mad at myself and then thought I didn't want to keep them anymore.

I get it, I say, and I do. But I wonder how we're going to pass the night.

⤞

Broomstick broken to a cudgel, held in an elderly woman's hand—old fat lady on the sidewalk. They are filming a series on the Avenue de Dame. Time was, nobody took pictures here. It's a sign of progress—at least that's what they say.

The woman crouches and collapses over the curb into a heap. Her body gives itself to the concrete in a way you'd not expect to see a living body do—loose as flour in a ten-pound sack. It's so convincing you would think she'd died. Her weapon sticks into a sewer, and all the other crap in the gutter, the mulch of leaves, the indistinct slop of too many rainy days, of too much exhaust paints her dress and her coat. Later, for the camera, they'll have her tear her dress and singe the hair growing out of her face. I think to myself, Someone's had to imagine this all, from the reek of engines to her bottle-cap knees, grinded into a curb before the open doors of the Marché aux Puces.

Spectators have lined up to watch. From across the street, behind barricades, they can hardly contain their excitement. They ask: Who do you think is the star of the show?

Who wrote the song I've been dreaming about?

What's the best place to hide a knife in the nude?

What's the best place to hide a bird?

Someone answers, In a cup of coffee, of course.

The director is watching it all on a screen. The writer is likely at home. It's gotten so suddenly cold, I forget to wear a sweater when I go for a walk. I try to be quiet, to make myself small. I squeeze by the caterer's table, careful not to upset the spread.

My friend is an avid reader, so I've picked up a copy of Donne's *Biothanatos*.

⤖

Now the man takes hold of his cock and my friend bites the tip of her tongue.

People wonder, he says, how a man can remain sensitive through the length of his life. He laughs. I don't know how others do, but I keep a tin of smelling salts, here in my pocket, in an old snuff box.

She mumbles and rolls onto her side, so he goes on telling a story.

Worse than her being unable to die, was the fact that she kept two dogs in a cage. She said she had to do it, or else when she left the house the dogs would tear into her memories. Her memories, she said, would be shredded, scattered all over the floor, but what could that mean? And what does a suicide want with her memories?

The accumulation of so many years, she offers.

The culmination of every awful thing that a person carries in this life: two desperate dogs locked into a box, says the man.

He scratches his face. My friend kicks the blankets off her toes.

In just another minute she'll start thinking aloud: The places you go—or more like the moments you live—or more like the ones that have passed—the moments of time—as if time was a clock—if a clock was a cage—and if we could only make more clocks, and carry clocks, and hang them on our kitchen walls— if only we could wear them on our wrists—clocks on fingers, clocks on doors—then by having so many, we'd be catching time, more and more and more of it, until the day came when we'd have gotten it—gotten it all and sealed it away. Then we'd be able to live our lives without time's abhorrent, constant convolution. We'd live one moment into the next—our lives a disconnected series of moments without the glue of time's narration to bind them.

They put the kettle on the stove to boil for tea.

After tea they climb into each other. Someone gets bitten and someone gets split. One gets an elbow, the other gets slapped. I roll my eyes across the bed and look to where the blankets hang down almost to the floor. On the floor is a stack of books. The one on top is *German Drama Between the Wars*. I roll my eyes and consider the sounds.

My friend turns onto her stomach and says, Pretend like I'm sleeping… She closes her eyes. If I were sleeping, what would you do?

I'm talking with the ghost of an old friend. She says to me, Give me a taste of your wasted thoughts.

Okay: Where's the best place to hide a bird? In a bowl of salt. Where's the best place to hide a knife? In a book no one'll read. Where's the best place to hide a fish? In your womb, of course. If you haven't got a womb, you find a girl, young man. Go find yourself a girl, give up everything you know for her. Give up all that made you whole and be a splintered bit of—shards of utter—bliss. Be a waste of passing days. Make a baby. Teach your baby right. Tie a pouch of smelling salts beneath his nose and tell him: Wear this for your whole long life. Should your baby be a lady, tell her: Always keep your eyes wide. Always keep your mind alert. But if your baby be a man, tell him: If you want hallucinations, sleep. If you want a transformation, dream. If you want to find a lover, sing. If you want to stay awake, my boy… To your daughters say: These salts will keep you active and give her a knife, saying: Where's the best place to hide a weapon? In the mail. Where's the best place to hide the truth? In the press. Where's the best place to hide around here?

Now the kid is driving around with our detective on the morning after the crime. He's narrating all of what happened before.

It was a birthday party, so we drank. We watched a woman dance. I was drunk.

What woman? asks the detective.

One woman, twice as old as the kid, gorgeous in the way she skipped around and around the stage.

Somewhere I wanted to put my teeth, says the kid, parked between her legs. Something hard to something soft. Something to drink, though I had drunken a lot.

They drive past the post office.

Here's where I sat and tried to carve our initials into wet cement.

Your own initial and those of a girl—but what girl?

I don't know. I remember her name, but that doesn't mean much.

The detective tells him, I'll decide what means what in all of this.

Here I crossed the street.

And why did you cross the street?

To run into someone.

And here again, says the kid, because it was getting cold and I saw some flowers. I wanted to bring those flowers home and give them to someone I knew.

To whom? the detective asks.

She doesn't live around here anymore.

The kid continues, I walked the rest of the way, admiring the petals, the leaves. Here I thought I would cut across the school-yard to gain a few minutes.

The detective pulls up across the street from his house. You live here by yourself? he asks.

No, says the kid, with a girl, but she's out of town right now.

I've got to come up, the detective says.

The way he sees: the stairs, the gauze-like shredded wool of wood, the empty rooms. How he detects subtlety, an abundance of lies, though not for lack of reaching toward the truth.

They walk into an empty room and the kids says, This is where we share our bed. We sleep together, my mine with her hers.

Into another empty room, the kid says, This is where we watch the news.

In the kitchen, a spoon, a piece of wood and a bowl. In the bathroom, the tap dripping into the tub. Steam across the vanity. No windows in the room.

Where did that bunch of flowers wind up?

I gave it away, says the kid, just like the Good Samaritan.

❧

At four o'clock in the morning, I take my son out for a walk. I carry him into alleyways and side streets. We count the doors hanging open like maws devouring the dark.

I say, One door.

He says, One.

I say, Two doors.

He says, Two.

I say, Three doors.

He says, Four doors, and it's startling to hear.

There is the image of a woman trying to catch letters from the alphabet as they crop into the frame around her bed. I see how easy it would be for the letter *e*, say, to be as sharp as ice when she grabs it. How she would be cut and would try then to rub out the pain of her fingers into her leg, not knowing that the glass had stuck into her skin. How she would open a new wound in her thigh.

The next time I look at my son, he's asleep. I am on my own now, carrying a child down the sidewalk of the Avenue de Dame. It's a portrait hanging crooked, but they're filming another episode here: a pair of drunks stand in a doorway and sing a soldier's lullaby while a worker cleans the sidewalk with hot water from a hose. Three men carry a wooden ladder down the street, taking breaks every so often. During their breaks, two of them kiss while the other stands with his back to the wall. They bare teeth into each other's mouths. They rub their legs together. Meanwhile the odd man out looks at his watch.

The truth is I don't care about any of this—not these people, nor their suffering, nor their sex. I lower my child into his bassinette and sing him into faraway sleep. I make myself a coffee and get ready for work.

☙

The man tells another story: Now he waits out the rest of the day for his girl to come home. He tries to sleep. He can't sleep. He spills a pile of dimes from a cup onto the floor. He turns on a light. The girl comes home after midnight, and that's it.

That's it? What happens? asks my friend.

It happens. I mean, he waited too long. There was no reason to wait. No reason to shake anymore. All the worst vibrations will rub themselves out, given time. They were both so tired, they fell asleep. Maybe in the morning, they fucked. He, having dreamt of a man with tattoos on his face and the door to their apartment wouldn't close. She dreamt of horses and of a poet with long, wavy hair. She'd had to sit with this woman for hours in a cellar, waiting for the end of a film.

I shuffle toward the window and think I see a pigeon in the dark, but it's a cluster of leaves, white and grey. Tell me, I ask the man myself. How does it feel to get older?

Older than what?

Older than me, I guess.

My friend hums the tune of a popular song called "Give a Young Man a Fish."

She sings, Beware of the fish, he'll swim into your life, and park himself high on a shelf with your books.

Now go to sleep, give it up, sleep until morning, till the mid-afternoon. When you are sick of it and feel you can't sleep anymore, sleep still a little while longer.

☙

She brings me to a place to play piano. We're under some building, in a padded room. We're here for an hour or more, the door latched shut behind our backs. We make a heap of our coats in the corner.

Her fingers, skeletal. Her arms, surreal. Her sense of how to usher in the silences, enviable in the highest degree. She tampers at the keys, non-committal. She ties strings together, each of them slack.

I ask, Who is the girl with dusty hair, ragged legs, long legs, ragged socks, knit sweater, hood up in the rain, rain water rolling over her eyelids? Same one who curls her arm to smoke?

I tell her, I want to carry on a dialogue with someone I've only just met, but she speaks a kind of gibberish.

It's supposed to be like piano keys, tampered in an empty room, the way one momentary hymn strikes up, collapses into another, lapses into some stutter of words, a note, a note, a cluster. Afterwards, grows into another hymn, different now, a bit of momentary still—as like the rise and fall of dunes in the desert. All the rest is just a mind that interferes. No one is asking anything when they've come to listen this way. The music she plays is interference. It makes them docile and content. It's enough for them to know that life is nothing but a series of this, strung end to end, nothing but a bundle of thread that's so loosely entwined and held, stuck together with crummy white glue. Problem is that my own composition is nothing but a stuttering of keys.

Later, I take her to the river. We walk for hours past factories, abandoned, red-bricked, out of use. You could pick up a rock and break windows. You could screw or go down to your knees. We do neither. We do nothing. We walk past broken doors.

She says, Do you want to go in?

I tell her I do, but we don't.

❧

She says to the man, Eat me where my limbs collide.

He does, and she accuses him thusly: I'm aware of what you'll say in the morning—either that vows made in wanting to fuck are like promises made to a mirror, or you'll say that as lust is to love, so sleep is to death, love lasting till death, lust only till sleep, and so in the morning is gone, and with it you go... I could argue, but why should I bother? Who knows if in the morning I won't feel the same way.

The kid spends his whole day in the bath. He drains a little water off and replenishes it so that the bath stays hot. He'll spend the whole night there as well, only going out once to meet a very tall man.

And I am still doing as I have done. Writing, *Here little bird, come take this bone and carry it with you wherever you go.*

Then like that, from fingers outstretched, palm to the ceiling, like releasing a dove or a pigeon, the very tall man bends himself into a ball and tries to hide in a corner of the room.

Every night I tell this story to my son before his going to bed: Once there was an old man with an apartment just north of the tracks who kept a flock of forty-four birds in his kitchen. (The detective pricks his ears, adjusts his ridiculous hat). But the birds never trusted the man. He fed them seeds which he had gathered with his own two hands and went about it with the gentleness of a man. The birds spent their lives near the ceiling—as far from the man as could be—treading in the air to keep themselves safe. Occasionally one or more would die of exhaustion, their paper-weight bodies falling to the kitchen floor. The man would sweep them up and carry them away. A funeral bath, the sashaying of a long woollen dress, black shoes, asphalt and yellow paint. (Then, all of a sudden, for having been so tall, the detective clews his body into a corner of the room. A girl dressed in mourning lies on the bed. Earlier today, she broke her favourite cup in the sink). Finally, the old man gets impatient. All he wanted was the loving respect of the birds, all he wanted was their trust. Now he feels cheated and betrayed. One day he tricks them out the window. They exit, and he closes it after them. It rains, and the birds are confused. Their wings, like leaves, drag them down in the cold.

By now my son is asleep, so I don't have to bother making sense of the tale.

The detective asks, How d'you like my hat?

A body washes up in the river. The paramedics jump out of their bus. One of them asks me, How it's going?

I tell him it's going alright.

My friend asks of her lover, What did you gain, trading one place for another?

He sits naked at the corner of her bed, his penis like a sock. I see he's got a tattoo on his outer thigh.

I was drinking too much. In addition to which I was young and proud and scared. Whenever I drank coffee, I was scared of death. When I smoked, I was scared of sex. I fell in and out of love, in and out of a woman's bed, scared of love, scared of life, scared of all the vibrating parts, the unaccomplished exorcism of my psyche, embarrassed by the crookedness of this, he says and gestures to his sock. This body of rotten leaves. This body electric, until after the rain. Etcetera, etcetera. Spending and fatigue. Departed and arrived. What's found is lost ...

We kill the lights.

There are words so personally dangerous they've got to be hidden in a litany of prose. That's when a writer has got too much to lose.

When I hold my child, I try to make my body soft for him, but my body isn't soft. It's full of bones held together by leathery skin. My son puts me into contact with my skeleton and I think of how awful it must feel. He sleeps on my chest, my chest made of bones.

I have seen the soft belly of a woman after everything is done—how fingers worked into the skin can make a river of the floor. Who will understand? My only explanation requires a story about a bottle and a cherry pit, but I can't remember sixty out of ninety of the words. Forget it. The town empties. Nobody makes a noise. Nothing but wait and see. Another night. And it's early November now.

A man went into the river in the broad light of the afternoon.

They say his penis was a purple flower, or a jelly bean, before he went under.

The next day a new series premiered, all about the lives of ordinary people in the neighbourhood. In the first episode, an elderly woman mails fifty-five copies of her house key to people in the town. She sits in a living room rocking chair with a photo album open on her lap. The pictures of her family, her husband, her children, her life, have her feeling bittersweet. She hears footsteps in the outer hall, but nobody opens the door. It's an episode of muted despair.

I wait three hours for my friend to arrive, forced in the meantime to listen to the man.

He says, The kid dreamt of a someone who would cross his path. That someone would be made of elephant tusks and the two of them would recognize each other immediately. The whole rest of the dream, the kid was trying to get back to his girlfriend's place. He needed to be certain that the door was locked because he knew now that the elephant being would be coming for them, carrying a knife to split 'em length-long and thin...

Ever since my friend got him talking, that man has been unable to stop. All his stories are empty now, or populated with reflections at best. I wonder if emptiness is catching. Finally I get bored and leave. I go to the river. Doors hang open on empty factories, on broken homes.

I ask, Should I go in?

The answer is yes.

꩜

At work, it's row by row. We go about our business and never
ask—

Now what was is flipped, and in the late afternoon I take a
bath without considering the light or time of day. I close the
bathroom door and shut the light within. I lie in the bath with
a washcloth over my eyes. I stay like that for God-only-knows,
could be the length of how many, so many instants lined up tit
to tail—could have been two hours, three months like that, lost
in no thinking at all.

After draining the bath, then towelling off, I'm surprised to
find the windows are dark. I am stunned, temporarily amazed.

Later I'll go for a walk, finding empty branches on every tree.

What's even more: the wind has stopped.

꩜

What happened?

Every drop of dreaming that I ever dreamt I did for you. I am
an empty shell—a limp dick, if you want. And all I ever learned
about the nature of a body, I learned it allegorically. I stood on
balconies, in bedrooms, in bathrooms, on the stairs. And it cost
a lot of blood in general, but none of it was mine. It cost me
almost nothing.

Meanwhile the town has gone musty, old, quiet—they say
it's less dangerous, but I'd still look out for certain narrow ways
on certain nights, for certain bars where certain bartenders pon-
tificate upon the nature of hell. It's become an awful bore, at any
rate. I'm just about ready to pack up my family and go.

The detective wants to know about the flowers.

The kid says, What's there to know?

He says he wants to know where'd you get the branch, and where did it go? Those sorts of things.

The kid answers with a question: Did you ever think of any-thing for such a long time, it left a blank spot in the centre of your head?

I climbed a set of stairs to get a vantage over the town. The truth is I know nothing about mystery though I have chased it in these streets. I was here for the conception of this, but I don't know how it happened. I can't make any sense of it.

My friend is in her kitchen. The man readies to go. She's untan-gling a thread, using the tip of a needle. She waits to hear his footsteps in the hall.

No one will bathe in her waters now. There'll be no one now to make sense of her skin, nor to silk the subtle floral of her moods, nor commit to her indifference.

What love doesn't do, she says, rage will create. What pain doesn't do, rage will invent.

She waits to hear the hard-heeled knock of a shoe beyond the door. He's ready to go.

You'll get wet, she says. It's raining.

I've been worse, says the man. When he goes, he leaves the door hanging open.

St. Henri, 2010

ACKNOWLEDGEMENTS

Thanks to everyone at Nightwood Editions who partici-
pated in the making of this book, to its editor Amber
McMillan, and especially to Silas White for the opportunity.

Thanks to the early readers of these stories for their insight
and encouragement, in particular to my parents Mary and Bob,
my uncle Stephen Laidlaw and to Nathan Szymanski.

Thanks to Andrew Szymanski, always my first and favourite
reader, long-time friend and partner in this (too often) miserable
effort at becoming writers.

Thanks to Janine for her continuous, invaluable support.

And to Janine for having sewn together, through all these
years, the fabric of a life with me.

And to Casper and Sebastian (bless their little hearts) for
doing as they ought to do—throwing wrench upon wrench
upon wrench into the gears.